Fires & Flamingos

The Chronicles of Addison Schmidt – Book One

Cassidy K. O'Connor

Fires & Flamingos

An Addison Schmidt Novel

Copyright ©2024

Published by: Celtic Hearts Press, LLC

Cover by: Crooked Sixpence Book Covers

Formatting by: Celtic Hearts Press, LLC

"FIRE!" Addison Schmidt ran out her front door, coughing as she ran a few feet away and glanced back. Smoke billowed out from the side of the house where the kitchen window was. "Damn it. I just repainted in there too."

Her next-door neighbor, Marilyn, the resident busy body stood in her yard with a hose, watering the plants she obsessed over. She shook her head at Addison. The woman could have acted a little more shocked. Then again, this was Addison's fifth fire in a month, so she had a reason to be exasperated instead of worried. She was at the point where she didn't even call to make insurance claims anymore. She couldn't afford the deductibles.

Addison screeched and flailed her arms around

when she noticed several strands of her hair were smoldering. "Oh my god... oh my god."

Marilyn smiled gleefully as she aimed the nozzle at Addison and soaked her.

Addison pushed her hair out of her face. "Really? You thought that was helpful?"

Marilyn shook her head as she chuckled. "I found it satisfying." Her lilting Scottish accent belied the nastiness of the woman. "I'll go call the fire department. You should marry one of them. It would get you a faster response time." As she set the hose down, water sprayed from it, whipping around the yard soaking her. "What..." she yelped as she ran for cover behind a tree, nearly tripping over one of the many plastic flamingos spread around her yard.

With Marilyn out of sight, the stream turned toward her. She ran at the hose and wrestled the nozzle to turn it off. It flopped to the ground for a second, then lifted to whip around again. Addison grabbed a rock from her garden, wrestled the hose to the ground again, and slammed the rock on the sprayer, pinning it down.

High-pitched barking coming closer meant her neighbor across the street, Cecil, and his dog Walter were coming over. Why did everything have to be a spectacle? Sometimes she was lucky and Cecil wouldn't have his hearing aids in, so he'd miss whatever mishap she was dealing with. But Walter the chihuahua had been outside, so of course he alerted Cecil. Just her luck.

Cecil hobbled across the street and clapped Allison on the back, sending her into another coughing fit. "What happened now?"

"Making Coffee." Addison wheezed out. Her throat raw from the smoke inhalation.

"You were raking softly?" His head tilted to the right in confusion.

"No making coffee." She enunciated every syllable.

"Baking barley?"

Okay, that didn't even make sense. Addison's shoulders dropped. She needed to carry around pen and paper so she didn't always go ten rounds with Cecil.

A soaking-wet Marilyn stomped over. "She was making coffee."

Cecil nodded. "Again?"

Addison huffed. Of course, he understood Marilyn on the first try. Everyone on the block knew Addison was no domestic goddess thanks to her little incidents, but he didn't have to seem like it was just another day in the neighborhood.

Walter growled before chomping down on the hose and pulling it from under the rock.

A thick stream of water arched its way toward Cecil. Addison jumped in front of him and took the worst of it. The jet of water turned again and aimed for Marilyn. Addison thought about jumping in front of her too, but the woman was already wet and maybe deserved it a little.

Addison ran over and wrestled the wriggling hose from Walter and shoved it under a bigger rock. She wagged her finger at Walter. "Leave it alone. That thing has a mind of its own."

The piercing sirens of the local fire department truck came rushing down the street. "Ugh." She hated it when the firemen showed up. They were all too young and gorgeous and she always looked her worst. The last time they had come she hadn't done laundry in a while, so she had been in an old college shirt that needed to be retired and made a rag, and sweatpants that were two sizes too big.

The first man off the truck was Captain Bill Handler. He shook his head at her as he walked by with the hose. "How many times a week are we going to do this? Why can't you just go to a coffee shop like everyone else?"

She scowled at him. He was getting paid to put out fires, not roast the residents.

Right behind him was Zeke Sizemore, with a fire extinguisher slung over his shoulder. The man was too good looking for his own good, and he knew it. He'd probably try to have a whole calendar with him shirtless every month if he could. Part of her would love to see that, but the strong-willed side of her wanted nothing to do with him.

"You know, if you want to ask me out, there are better ways to do it than setting your house on fire." He winked as he passed her. She inhaled and growled. Why did he have to smell good, too?

The last one off the truck was a young female firefighter. She dug around a compartment on the side of the truck and walked over to hand Addison a small blanket. "You might want this." She nodded her head toward Addison's chest.

Addison glanced down and gasped. Her thin tank top was plastered to her body. Even worse, it's what she slept in, so no bra underneath. She wrapped herself in the blanket and spun around to Marilyn. "Don't you know girl code? You should have told me I was showing off my chesticles."

"What about testicles?" Cecil interjected.

Addison growled and stomped away. She didn't have patience for either of them right now.

Zeke walked out, pulling the hose behind him. "You're in luck. It was a small fire this time." He noticed the blanket. "You know I get off at seven if you want to get a drink."

It took the man seeing her headlights to get him to ask her out. She didn't care how long it had been since she'd had sex. Zeke was not getting the chance to put out her fire with his hose.

two

ADDISON STOOD in the doorway of the kitchen. After all the drama with the fire the day before, she'd had to rush to her job, ironically at the coffee shop, and by the time she'd made it home, she'd been too tired to clean anything. Lucky for her, the fire was able to be put out with the extinguisher so there was no water damage this time.

In the bright morning light, it was a relief to see the damage wasn't as bad as she thought it would be. Luck was on her side again.

The cute curtains with little cherries on them were barely recognizable, though. They were one of her first purchases after her divorce and had survived all the previous fires.

Her ex, Jerry, liked everything orderly and classy.

No frilly holiday decorations or whimsical curtains for him. Now that she was newly single, she'd made sure every room of the house was splashed with color or had a funny sign somewhere. Her favorite was in her laundry room. The sign read, "The laundry is looking *dirty* at me again". That one made her chuckle every time.

The bright teal of the cabinets still made her smile when she saw them. Jerry would have hated them. Her sons tried to talk her out of them, talking about hurting the resale value, but she was on her own for the first time in her life with no one else to compromise with.

Sure, she might have taken her decorating a bit too far, like when she'd changed all the hanging lights in the house into disco balls. She'd only done it because the boys had been so against them. The lights didn't last long, though. Even she thought they were tacky and when the sun bounced off them, she'd gotten a headache.

The high school drama department had loved it when she donated them, along with some weird fruit-shaped couch pillows she'd bought. Their prop department had almost doubled its size since she'd moved in.

She didn't have any guilt over the repeated

remodels, either. Most were necessary because of the accidents and it was her alimony money from Jerry that paid for every item he would have hated.

She could get by with just the alimony, but the coffee shop gave her a place to go and a nice cushion in her bank account.

The front door creaked open. That was a new quirk, since whatever was going on with her had started two months ago. The trouble began when she noticed things she'd thought about would manifest. It was little things like when she thought she had finished her coffee, but it was full again. She'd thought she was losing her mind.

Next came the lights going on and off as she moved from room to room. While vacuuming, she had somehow managed to send the couch sliding across the room and smashed it against the entryway. Since then, the door groaned every time it was opened, as if it were sore.

She peeked around the corner and sighed. Her oldest son, Fritz, stood in the doorway. She had named him during her F. Scott Fitzgerald period. She had been reading The Great Gatsby when she'd gone into labor.

Fritz held up a melted coffee pot. "Again? Seriously?"

"It was time for a new coffeemaker, anyway." She shrugged nonchalantly.

"One of these days you're going to burn the whole house down." He chucked the burned appliance onto the porch where it lay dejectedly with the other coffee makers, toaster, and hair dryer that had all spontaneously combusted. The screen door banged behind him as he went inside.

"That will just mean I can redecorate again. I am still trying to figure out my style. I like the challenge of trying something new each time."

"Mom. Why can't you take this seriously? Something is going on with you and I don't like it. If you're not more careful, you could get seriously hurt. And when are you going to get rid of all that junk?"

She hated seeing the fear in his eyes. She sighed. "I promise I am taking this seriously. I don't know what's going on, but I am trying to be careful." That was a lie. She suspected what was happening, but it was too crazy to even consider. "I keep hoping the other appliances will behave if they see the graveyard of those that came before them." His jaw dropped. "I'm kidding. I saw a sign in town about someone buying used appliances. I keep meaning to take all that stuff there, but haven't gotten around to it yet."

Fritz opened his mouth to reply, but paused when someone knocked loudly on the frame of the screen door. They both turned and cocked their heads. Marilyn stood on the porch holding a paper up. She was gripping it so tight it shook.

Addison did not want to deal with the ornery woman at that moment, but she knew she had no choice. She pasted on a bright smile and pushed the screen door open. "Marilyn, so good to see you again." The sweetness dripped off every word.

The other woman thrust the paper at Addison. "Here."

Addison scanned it. "Are you asking me to pick up your dry cleaning for you?"

Marilyn's scowl deepened. "I want you to pay for it. Those are the clothes I had on yesterday when your little fire happened."

Addison snorted. "You were working in your garden. Surely your clothes weren't so nice that you needed to have them dry-cleaned?"

Marilyn gasped. She was clearly offended by Addison's implication. "I beg your pardon. You are not the fashion police. Just get me my money." She sniffed as if the smoke smell was still attached to Addison.

Marilyn toed the pile of burned appliances. "Such a menace. One of these days, you're going to burn the whole neighborhood down. You're just lucky none of your drama has impacted my award-winning rose bushes, or you'd have a lawsuit on your hands."

The paper in Addison's hand crumpled in the fist she was making. "Thank you, Marilyn. You can leave my property now. I wouldn't want anything bad to happen to you."

The older woman had no idea how true that statement was. Things Addison thought tended to come true.

Marilyn clutched her chest. "My word. So rude." She spun on her heel and stomped down the drive-way, muttering as she passed the vehicles that had pulled up.

Addison's other two sons had wisely stayed in their cars until the coast was clear. They were likely there to lecture her, too. They didn't get the memo about who the parent was in their relationship.

She took a few steps across the yard to wait for them, but stopped short when she saw a man standing across the street. The handsome stranger was wearing a suit that screamed 'I'm rich, come rob me'. He definitely didn't belong in their quiet little neighborhood.

By the time she made it back up to his face, she jumped when she saw he was staring intently back at her. Now she wished she was wearing anything nicer than the sweats she had put on to clean her burned kitchen.

"Yo, mom. You okay?" Her second born, Leo, named after Leonardo DaVinci because she watched the movie Mona Lisa with Julia Roberts three times while she was in labor with him, stood in front of her, waving his hand in front of her face.

Something about the man across the street had her distracted. His perfectly tailored suit hinted at the muscular man underneath. As if it were the 1950s again, he reached up and grabbed the rim of his fedora hat and tipped it.

What in the name of time travel was this?

"She is seriously zoned out." Iggy, her third born, named after Iggy Pop, which she listened to on repeat during her punk rock phase, mumbled.

"Mom!" Iggy and Leo yelled at the same time.

She finally broke eye contact with the stranger and gave each son a quick hug. "Hang tight. I need to catch up to Marilyn. No way am I paying for her dry cleaning. It was her hose that went crazy, not mine."

Leo grabbed her arm as she tried to walk around them. "Wait. We wanted to catch you up on who we're dating right now."

She squinted at them. They never wanted to talk about their love lives. Try setting them up a couple of times and suddenly you are blacklisted. Was it her fault the barista she set Fitz up with had talked about what their kids would look like while they were on their first and only date? Or the cashier from the grocery store who ended up being sixteen while Leo was twenty-eight.

"Come inside so we can talk about it," Iggy added.

Addison nodded. "This better be good. Come on, I have iced tea in the fridge."

As she followed her boys inside, she took one last look across the street, but the gorgeous man was nowhere to be seen. She glanced up and down the street. Had she only imagined him? Stranger things had happened lately.

three

ADDISON FLEW OUT of bed as the acrid smell of smoke tickled her nose. "What the hell? I wasn't even awake this time." She ran down the hall, going through the routine she did every night before bed. Had she forgotten to turn something off? It wasn't the coffee maker since she hadn't replaced the last one yet.

She bounded around the corner into the kitchen and screamed. It took a few heartbeats for her to realize the man across from her wasn't a stranger trying to break in.

Cecil stood at her stove in his striped pajama bottoms and a robe. He was oblivious to her as he hummed as he burned French toast on the griddle.

She glanced at the door leading out the side of

the house and noticed it was still locked. She spun around and gasped. The front door was wide open. "Now I know I locked that last night." It was always the last thing she did before bed.

She stomped over to Cecil and tapped his shoulder. "Cecil, what are you doing here?"

He jumped and spun around. The hot, very melted spatula in his hand barely missed her face. She cleared her throat when she noticed he didn't have a shirt on and his robe was open. For an older man, he was still surprisingly fit. His chest and belly were smooth except for the happy trail leading down from his belly button. It could be a trick of the light, but it looked like he might have a couple of abs too. Not a whole six-pack, just two or three cans, and that wasn't bad for a man in his eighties.

She looked away and tried to clear her mind. If Cecil was looking good to her, she was in serious need of getting laid, and not by him.

"Addison, what are you doing in my kitchen? You scared the dickens out of me," Cecil demanded.

Her jaw dropped. "Your kitchen? You're in my house?"

He cupped his free hand behind his ear. "Say what?"

Instead of repeating herself, she grabbed his arm

and led him to the living room. "This is my house." She pointed out the front door. "Your house is over there."

His cheeks pinkened as his shoulders sagged. "I'm sorry. I don't know why I'm here."

She could hear the frustration and dejection in his voice. The poor man really shouldn't be living alone. "Since you're here, do you want to stay for breakfast? You did make it after all."

He chuckled as he nodded. "Yes, please."

Oh sure. He heard that.

She led him to a kitchen chair and grabbed some plates out of the cabinet. "Wait. Where's Walter?"

"What's that?"

She took a deep breath and raised her voice. "I'm going to your house to get your hearing aids and to check on Walter."

"Okay, okay. You don't gotta yell."

She bit her lip before saying something rude and rushed to her bedroom. She tossed on a sweatshirt and flip-flops and made her way out of the house.

She made it two steps out the door when a searing pain in her head had her doubling over. It felt like a vice grip and a poker stabbing her at the same time.

She groaned as she massaged her scalp. As if her

morning weren't bad enough, Marilyn's whiny voice reached her.

"You aren't cooking again, are you? Do I need to call the fire department?" The older woman stood on her porch with her hands on her hips.

Addison's stomach rolled as she stood back up. A flash of something in her driveway caught her eye. She held her hand up to cover the sun shining in her eyes. She swore she saw the stranger from the day before. It must have been her imagination.

Marilyn's grating voice followed Addison as she rushed across the street. The pain in her head wasn't subsiding. If she passed out in front of Marilyn, the woman would probably call an ambulance. Addison didn't need that drama, too.

"Why are you going to Cecil's?" Marilyn shouted.

Addison turned to wave her off and missed the curb. Her toes crunched against the cement as she flew forward onto her hands and knees. "Mother-fu–" She pushed to her feet and brushed off her skinned knees. No cute dress for her today.

She made it to Cecil's front door and paused when she saw the state of the porch. Spread around was a laundry basket, a pile of unopened canned baked beans, and a bottle of shampoo.

Maybe he was worse off than she thought. Her next day off she was going to have to stop over and check on things.

Marilyn's shrill voice was even closer. "Wait, you can't go in there."

Addison spun around. Marilyn stood on the sidewalk holding her obnoxious cat, Cleopatra. The little diva hellion was as annoying as her owner was. She loved escaping her house, perching on Addison's windowsill, and yowling her loudest. She'd never wished harm on an animal before, but some days Cleopatra toed the line.

Addison raised her arm and pointed to her neighbor's lawn. "Don't you have anything better to do than harass people? Go plant something."

As the sentence died off her lips, a loud boom echoed down the street. Smoke plumed from Marilyn's front yard so thick she could barely see the older woman any longer.

If she hadn't seen it personally, she would never have believed the chaos that ensued next.

Cleopatra screeched, which was quickly replaced by Marilyn's scream.

"Fuck. What now?" Addison just wanted one peaceful day. Why was that so hard to get?

One day, when no emergencies or annoying

neighbors were harassing her. Was it too much to ask for a handsome man to show up and screw her into oblivion? The image of the well-dressed stranger popped into her head. Yeah, he'd do nicely.

She jogged across the street, ignoring the other neighbors coming out to watch the spectacle. She waved her arm to clear the smoke and almost tripped over Marilyn, who was sitting on the ground sobbing. "Cleo!"

How did she go from searching for a dog to now looking for a cat? And somehow she'd lost a flip-flop too. "It's okay. I'm going to find her. Hang on."

Marilyn lifted a shaky hand and pointed toward her house.

Addison turned and fell on her ass next to Marilyn. "What the actual fuck?"

There, standing in the center of Marilyn's lawn, was an eight-foot-tall, neon-pink plastic flamingo.

four

ADDISON STOOD at her kitchen window, staring at the giant flamingo in her neighbor's yard. It had been twenty-four hours, and she still had no idea where Cleopatra went, where the plastic yard ornament had come from, or how Cecil had gotten into her house.

The chaos of her life was bleeding over onto those around her, and that was never good.

Addison's sons had called one after another to offer their ideas of what had happened. None of them believed she wasn't involved. Iggy had begged her to tell him where she got the giant flamingo from and Leo tried to say it was likely aliens doing social experiments on them. He always had the wildest imagination.

She still hadn't forgiven them for tricking her into her house the other day to talk about dating, and once they were inside, they changed the subject. They had been so afraid of her going after Marilyn that they played on her emotions to get her inside.

The impertinence of her children.

To make matters worse, Cecil's grandson was the new chief of police and he called asking her to come to the station for an interview when she got off work. At least he had softened the request by first thanking her for getting his grandfather back home.

Cecil had been so agitated and embarrassed about showing up in her kitchen, but once she got him home and they found Walter hiding under the bed, he'd settled down.

She glanced over at the empty spot on the counter where her coffee pot had been. How was she going to explain any of this and not sound certifiable?

The creak of the front door pulled her out of her morose thoughts. "Come on back. I'm in the kitchen." She yelled out, wondering which son was popping by for another "random" visit.

She put two cups of instant coffee in the microwave before turning to greet her visitor.

Her heart jumped when she saw the stranger

who'd been lurking outside her house standing in the doorway. He was real.

She reached behind her and grabbed the first thing her hand touched. The wooden spoon wouldn't have been her first choice, but sometimes you gotta do what you gotta do. "Who are you, and why are you in my house?"

He smirked at her feeble attempt to intimidate him. "My name is Xavier. I'm a paranormal investigator. Your door was cracked open, and you called out, inviting me in."

She swung the spoon toward the front door. "It wasn't open. That invitation was for my sons. And I don't want anything you're selling."

He held his hands up in an attempt to seem less threatening.

News flash, it wasn't working.

He pulled a short but impressively thick notebook out of his jacket pocket. "An irate customer talked backward for forty-eight hours after a confrontation with you. The store where you get your wine was out of stock and the next day they got four semi truckloads of the one kind you were looking for. You probably have a hundred crazy stories that no one else will believe. But I will." He waved one hand toward a kitchen chair. "May I sit?"

The idea of someone, anyone, believing her was too much to pass up. What if he had the answers to what was happening around her? "Move slowly and keep your hands flat on the table."

She was very proud of herself for her tough-girl act. If only he knew she was freaking out and thanks to her forty-six-year-old bladder, he had literally scared a little piss out of her.

"I was in town investigating some strange occurrences when I was drawn to your block. As I followed the energy, it intensified as it led me straight to you. It didn't take me long to figure out you are completely unaware of what's happening, and that makes you dangerous."

Not wanting to show any fear, she laughed loudly. "I don't know what you're talking about. I've had some bad luck lately and my clumsiness has reached a new high, but it's all explainable." She shot to her feet, the spoon still in hand, and promptly tripped over the leg of the table. "See what I mean? And I mean yeah, fires keep breaking out. It happens with older houses. I need to have an electrician come out. And sure, my lawn mower seemed to have a mind of its own when it ran over Marilyn's bushes, but the safety bar had gotten stuck and I couldn't get to it in time."

"What about Cleopatra and the flamingo?" He asked dryly.

She huffed as she plopped into her chair. "I don't know where she is. The entire neighborhood has been looking for her. I made all kinds of flyers." She chose to ignore the giant flamingo that showed up exactly when Cleopatra disappeared.

"Can I tell you a story?" He waited for her to nod. "A couple of years ago, I was sent to Milwaukee to help a woman who thought she was going insane. She had the same strange phenomena happening. There was so much she refused to believe. Her complete denial of the truth proved to be too much. She took her own life. It was my first major failure. I don't want the same thing to happen to you."

Addison gulped. Why had she let this stranger in and why did she listen to him? "Listen, my husband is going to be home soon, and he's the jealous type. I think you should go before he gets here."

Xavier crossed his arms. "Liar."

"Excuse me?" She scowled at him. "And don't think I didn't notice you moved your hands." She waved the spoon at him again.

"You're divorced. Something triggered all this. Let me guess, you're able to make objects move with a simple word, and you can turn things on and off by simply saying 'turn on' or 'turn off'."

Addison gasped. How did he know she was her own personal Alexa? No one had ever seen her do any of those things, not even her sons.

She set the spoon down and ran her hands through her hair. She was trying hard not to freak out. She studied Xavier's face. He never wavered. Maybe he was there to help her. "I don't know what's happening. My kitchen keeps catching fire-"

"You're on your third coffee maker." He interjected.

"My neighbor Cecil showed up inside my locked house-"

"In his pajamas, making breakfast." He finished her sentence.

"I don't think Cleopatra is missing. I think I turned her into an eight-foot-tall-"

"Flamingo," He mumbled as he scribbled words in his notebook.

How did he know all of this? Addison licked her lips as her eyes darted toward the front door. She'd give anything for one of her sons to show up for their good-intentioned welfare checkup. All of this was too much, and she needed Xavier gone. Her chest tightened as it got harder to take deep breaths.

Was it too late to move to a desolate island and forget any of this happened?

Xavier must have noticed she was close to freaking out. He quickly put his notebook away and sat back. His eyes slid up and down her body. A single drop of sweat rolled down her spine.

"I believe you have latent magic abilities, and I don't think the divorce caused them to come to the surface. I think it was when you started menopause."

Addison's jaw dropped. "What the… how dare you. I am *not* menopausal." He lifted one eyebrow at her. "I'm perimenopausal, Mr. Know it all. There is a big difference between the two thank you very much. Not that I need to explain any of that to you. It's none of your business." Heat rushed through her body. The worst part was she didn't know if it was from nerves or a hot flash. "And magic? What in the Harry Potter are you talking about? None of that is real. I don't have any magic."

Would that explain everything? Sure. Was she ready to accept it? Abso-freaking-lutely-not.

Xavier pushed up from the table. "I'm sorry if I offended you. I'll take my leave now."

Addison wilted in relief. This had been the strangest morning in a long line of strange mornings. She walked him to the door. "I'm sorry you wasted your time coming here. Have a nice life."

She closed the door on his retreating back and forcefully turned the deadbolt. When she went to the store for another coffee maker, she was definitely picking up a chain lock. She may be ready to have men visit her, but first Cecil and now Xavier coming in uninvited was not her idea of a good time.

five

ADDISON STARED up at the ceiling fan. She'd been lying there for the last two hours with her mind racing. Was Xavier right? Magic couldn't be real, could it? It would be great if it was true. That would explain all the chaos. If she was magical, where did it come from? The scariest question of all… if magic was real, was it going to drive her insane if she didn't deal with it?

A noise outside her window snapped her out of her thoughts. "What now?" She couldn't remember the last time she had one whole normal day, and this one was starting in the early morning hours and she had the early shift at the coffee shop.

The dark was something she'd never been a fan of. It was even worse now that she lived alone. She'd been with her husband for twenty-six years. This was the only time she missed him... when there was a noise outside and someone had to investigate.

She said 'turn on' as she went from room to room. As a last-second thought, she saw her trusty wooden spoon on the counter and grabbed it for protection. It may be time to look into something a little scarier.

She waited for the entire backyard to be lit up before she stepped outside. "Seriously? Again?"

The noise was coming from someone on their hands and knees rustling through her shrubs. She'd recognize those pajamas anywhere. "Cecil." She sighed as she went back to the front of the house to slip on her sneakers.

She rushed out the back door and skidded to a stop. Xavier, still looking fantastic in his fancy suit, stood with an arm around Cecil's shoulders. The pair were walking toward the side yard as Cecil mumbled about Walter.

Her heart broke for him. Confusion was hard enough to deal with, but losing his companion had to be even harder on him.

Not sure why Xavier was there and what he was doing with her neighbor, she chased after them.

She caught up as they crossed the street. "Why are you here?"

He kept Cecil moving forward as he answered. "I'll explain after."

That's the best she would get at two a.m.?

Addison rushed ahead to open the door for them. A quick glance confirmed not much had changed on the porch. A new addition was a gallon of milk on the railing.

She let Xavier pass with Cecil and, as a last-second thought, she grabbed the milk to dump it. The last thing she needed was Cecil trying to drink it.

Addison handed Xavier the jug. "Hold this and don't move." No way was she letting him into Cecil's house.

She peeked in the first door on the right and found it was the master bedroom. Cecil mumbled again about Walter. The little troublemaker crawled out from under the bed and barked at them.

"Seriously? I'm going to block that space off so you can't hide under there anymore." She settled Cecil in bed and picked up Walter. "I don't know if you are allowed to sleep in the bed, but he needs you right now, so stay put until morning."

Walter turned his head as if he was listening. Wouldn't that be nice?

She went back to Xavier and grabbed the bottle. "Give me a minute." She went to the kitchen sink, opened the bottle, and gagged. How had it gone bad so fast? She covered her face with her shirt, hoping it would block some of the smell, and dumped as quickly as she could. For good measure, she squeezed dish soap in the sink and ran the garbage disposal.

When her eyes had stopped watering from the stench, she grabbed the cell phone she knew Cecil had for emergencies and called the first number programmed in his favorites.

"Hello?" a groggy voice answered.

"Chief Novak, this is Addison Schmidt."

He cut her off. "When I asked for an interview, I didn't mean on my personal cell in the middle of the night. Wait, why are you calling from my grandfather's phone? Did something happen?"

"Nothing serious, but I found him in my back-yard crawling around the bushes." She heard him sigh. "Xavier and I walked him back to the house, and he's back in bed."

"Is Xavier another neighbor?"

"No. I just met him a couple of days ago. He's tall

with black hair and blue eyes. He wears very snug business suits that really show off his muscular frame. And don't get me started on the hat. It's old school, but I kind of like it."

"This isn't a dating service. I don't need that much detail."

Addison's cheeks burned. Why did she say all that? How did she explain so he didn't think she was a love-sick teen? "I'm telling you in case something happens to me. I don't know this man, and it's the middle of the night."

"I see. I'm coming over now. I'll stay the rest of the night to make sure he doesn't wander again. Thank you for watching out for him. You keep rescuing him even though he isn't your burden."

She felt bad for both men, but especially Theo. He was so young to deal with this, but his parents were gone, so he had to take responsibility. "It's okay. Cecil is a wonderful man. I feel for him and I'm worried about his safety."

"I know. I'll have to move him soon. I'm just not ready to take him from everything he knows."

This was a deeply personal conversation to have with a stranger. He must have been lonely if he was telling her. "I'll see you when you get here."

She ended the call and put the phone back on the charger where she found it.

Xavier sighed as she walked back to the front door. "That man should not be living alone."

Addison nodded her agreement. "Shall we?" She shooed him out of the doorway. "Well, thank you for the help. Have a good night."

She plopped down on the top step to wait for Theo.

Xavier gracefully sat next to her. "I've been thinking about our conversation. If you are adamant the magic isn't coming from you, then there must be something in your house that is causing these magical events. It's not safe for you if so."

She still wasn't ready to accept magic was real, so she stayed silent.

"I couldn't sleep worrying about you, so I popped by to make sure everything was okay. When I saw your neighbor going around the side of your house, I thought I'd get him before he scared you and you attacked him with your wooden spoon."

"Hey, that spoon could be deadly if I wanted it to be." He seemed genuinely concerned for her, though. "You can see I'm okay. I appreciate you checking on me."

"I'd like to look around your house and see if I

spot anything unusual?" She opened her mouth to object, but he pushed on. "We're both awake and I'm here. It won't take long. If I don't find anything, you'll never see me again."

This was crazy. "The first time you were in my house was a fluke because I thought you were one of my kids. Now you expect me to invite you inside in the middle of the night?"

"I can come back during the day if that would make you feel better but we're both awake now and given the head of the police is going to be across the street and you told him all about me I think you'd feel better doing it now?"

She hesitated a moment before nodding. No matter what, she had to get control of these powers, and Xavier was likely the person to help her. "Fine. But I swear to all that is holy, if you try anything, I'll turn you into an eight-foot-tall flamingo."

"So you do have magic?"

She glared at him. "Touche"

They sat silently for a few minutes until a police car pulled up and backed into the driveway.

Addison and Xavier walked to the edge of the grass and waited. The tall and ridiculously good-looking sheriff got out of the car and grabbed a duffle bag out of the backseat.

She held her hand out. "It's nice to officially meet you, Chief Novak."

His warm hand firmly grasped hers. "Please. You've rescued my grandfather enough to call me Theo." He raked his eyes over Xavier. "Addison's description of you was on par. Thank you for helping them."

Xavier nodded his head in return. "Not a problem at all."

They parted ways and crossed the street back to Addison's house. She paused at the door. "I'm not kidding. The chief has seen your face and has the skill and law behind him to kill you if you do anything to me." That threat felt a lot better than her wooden spoon.

six

ADDISON SAT at the kitchen table and watched as Xavier went over every inch of the kitchen. He was meticulous. More than once, she worried he was going to find a dust bunny or something gross. She was a clean person, but she probably wasn't white glove ready and Xavier was definitely going that deep in his check of the house.

In one hand, he had a small black box which had a row of flashing lights that never seemed to change. From the other hand hung a chain with a blue stone at the end. Sometimes he'd put one down to feel around areas he couldn't see well.

She finally couldn't stand the silence any longer. "So, whatcha doing?"

He stayed under the cabinet as he answered.

"I'm doing a few things. I'm using my eyes to look for anything suspicious. This meter will alert me if anything from another plane of existence is near. And this charm will glow if another magical object is nearby."

She thought about asking him if the charm would glow next to her, but figured that was admitting she might be accepting this magic he said she had.

Maybe if she didn't talk, he would finish faster and leave. Her alarm was going to be going off much sooner than she'd like. She was an eight-hours-a-night kind of girl and since the coffee machines had broken twice when she was using them, her boss had her on cleaning duty instead, which always made her day a little worse. She didn't know why they were so grumpy. At least the machines didn't catch fire.

More than once, she'd nodded off and woke up to drool on her chin. Wiping her jaw made her remember she'd missed her last chin waxing appointment. If she didn't get there soon, she was going to grow a beard and then no man would want to date her.

Her cell phone rang, causing them to jump.

"You get calls at three in the morning?" Xavier

questioned.

She shook her head. Her stomach dropped when she saw it was her son, Leo. He'd never called her in the middle of the night before. Her hand shook as she answered. "What's wrong?"

"Grandma and I are okay, but there is something weird going on and you have a lot of weird stuff going on, so I was hoping you'd come over and take a look?" Leo didn't sound like his usual chill self.

"I'll be there in fifteen." She hung up and stood quickly. "My son lives above my mother's garage and he needs me to come over."

"Do you need me to come?" He looked genuinely concerned.

As much as she wanted to have a man to lean on again, she wasn't going to fall into that trap again. "It's okay. I've got it. I'll leave you here to finish, but I'm warning you, I have nanny cams all over the house."

She didn't actually have cameras, although as a single female, it probably wasn't a bad idea. She made a mental note to look into them later.

Still dressed from taking Cecil home, she gave Xavier the 'I'm watching you' gesture by pointing at her eyes and then him.

He rolled his eyes and chuckled. "I'll be on my

best behavior. If you do end up needing anything, call me." He jotted down a number on the back of a receipt he'd had in his pocket and handed it to her.

She glanced at the front of the receipt and lifted an eyebrow at him.

"What?"

"You eat like a five-year-old. Chocolate milk and glazed donuts?" It sounded like the perfect breakfast to her, but she had to give him a hard time first.

He shrugged. "I'll die a well-fed, happy man. I have no regrets."

"Hhmp. Must be nice." and she meant it. She had so many it was embarrassing to think about. Staying in her marriage once the kids were grown was regret number one.

She shook her head. "Crap. I gotta go." Something about that man sucked her right in. He was going to be dangerous for her heart if she wasn't careful.

Her fingers ached from grasping the steering wheel as she drove to her mother's house. At least she knew everyone was okay, so she didn't have to speed. Before her divorce, she was super unhappy, but life was calm and insanely boring. Since she'd been on her own, it had been nothing but peri-menopause and chaos. It was probably a good thing it all started after she left Jerry. He would not have tolerated her mood swings well and an unhappy Jerry meant everyone was unhappy.

When she pulled up to her childhood home, she found them sitting on the front porch.

Her mother, Theresa, handed her a cup of coffee. "I figured you might need this with us waking you up in the middle of the night."

Addison normally wouldn't have drunk it, but she really hadn't been to bed yet and still had a handsome stranger at her house, likely robbing her blind. She definitely wasn't going to tell them that, though. Instead, she took a big gulp. "Okay. Show me what's going on."

Theresa's hand shook as she reached for the doorknob and opened the front door. "It's the damnedest thing. I came downstairs because I forgot to take one of my pills and almost crapped myself when I saw this." She waved her arm around the living room as they walked in.

Addison gasped. "Leo, when you said weird, you were seriously understating this."

Every wall and piece of furniture was covered

with black symbols with scorch marks. They weren't anything she recognized, but even with her baby toe barely in the magic pool, she could feel something radiating off them. Power maybe? This was her first time sensing something from another object or person. Maybe she was magical, and this was her recognizing something else magical? It would be kind of cool to be a witch, or would she be a sorceress? That sounded cooler. Where did you even find out something like that?

As her fingers traced along the nearest symbol, what felt like static electricity came off the mark and stung her. Each one looked like it was burned into the surface and left ash behind. "Do you remember seeing this room before you went to bed? You know they weren't here?"

Theresa nodded. "I sat in here watching TV until midnight, then went to bed. The room was completely normal."

Addison turned to Leo. He was always up late. "So sometime between midnight and three a.m. someone came in here and did this. You don't remember hearing or seeing anything?"

He shook his head. "No, but I also had my headset on and I was playing a game on my computer. I checked her doorbell camera, and it didn't show anyone coming in or out."

Addison had a sinking feeling this had to do with whatever was happening to her. She walked around and took meticulous pictures of every symbol. If nothing else, she'd show Xavier and see if he had any ideas.

Headlights of a car pulling up to the house distracted her. "Do you have a gentleman caller we don't know about?"

Theresa snorted. "I'll leave the dating to you. Leo called the non-emergency police line. We wanted to have this on record in case anything else happened."

She had no doubt the cops were going to be useless in this situation. Until she accepted maybe she had magic and shared it with her family, she'd have to go along with the possibility of this being a prank. Deep down, she knew this wasn't innocent. Whoever did this was a threat to her and her family.

ADDISON WAS EXHAUSTED. After the polite but unconcerned police left her mother's house, she ran home to shower, get real clothes on, and make sure Xavier hadn't robbed her.

He hadn't. He did leave a note saying he hadn't found anything and to call if she needed help with whatever happened at her mother's house.

She sighed as she tossed her phone in the cupholder of her car. Her boss hadn't been happy she called out, but there was no way she could work when she was going on twenty-six hours awake. Plus, she wanted to get the room cleaned up so her mom could forget about it faster.

One more quick trip to check on her mom, then

she'd go home and sleep. She had a date later and would not let some hocus pocus derail that.

A bit of her worry eased as she pulled into the driveway and saw her mother's house looked calm and still in one piece. She felt terrible that her mom was so upset. She had a right to be. The idea of someone being in your house while you slept was terrifying. Addison had to find a way to keep her family from getting involved in her mess.

The smell of bacon led her to the kitchen. Leo stood at the stove cooking over medium eggs. "Welcome back. You're just in time."

"Where's grandma?" The rest of the house was dark and quiet.

"She fell asleep as soon as you left. She asked me to hang here until she woke up." He sighed as he sat down with the plate of eggs. "I feel so bad that I missed whatever happened last night. You always said I got too consumed when I played. I guess you were right."

She reached across the table and squeezed his hand. "This is not on you. This is on whatever creeper came in here trying to scare your grandmother. Nothing physically happened to her, so we'll count our blessings and be more vigilant, right?"

Leo nodded and then smirked. "What if the house is haunted, and a ghost did it? Maybe they're trying to tell us something." Addison paused to consider the idea until she saw Leo's face turn to shock. "You don't seriously think ghosts are real, do you?"

Addison snorted. "No. Of course not."

Um, yeah, she did.

Or maybe Xavier had something to do with it. How odd of him to come around in the middle of the night and keep her busy at the same time this was happening at her mom's.

Wait... that didn't make sense. Why would it matter if she was distracted when the vandalism was happening miles away?

Leo looked appeased at her answer. "Maybe if we research the symbols that will lead us to some gang or something?"

"That's exactly why I took so many pictures." She highly doubted it had anything to do with gangs, at least not the human kind.

He held his phone up, showing he took a picture of one of the symbols. "I googled this one, and it kept coming back with something about dark magic or something. We should call like a psychic or something."

"Absolutely not. The police are handling this, and I'll do some research on the side." She got up to clean the table and then turned quickly back to Leo. "Let's keep this in the immediate family. Your dad doesn't need to know any of this. Not that he cares about me or grandma but I still don't want him in our business."

Leo rolled his eyes. "Yeah, yeah. I know."

She felt bad as she stood, filling the dishwasher. Her sons had all been supportive when she decided to leave their dad. They could see how small and insignificant she'd become. After so many years of unhappiness, she had retreated in on herself and hadn't even realized it. It wasn't like Jerry was cruel or abusive. He was the complete opposite. He had zero feelings toward her and most of the time acted like she didn't exist. It wasn't like that in the beginning. With each kid, she saw him retreating more and more. She wasn't even sure what it was that finally snapped her out of it.

Once the kitchen was clean, they grabbed cleaning supplies from under the sink and went to tackle the markings.

Addison started on one side, and Leo on the other. Symbol after symbol stubbornly withstood every bit of scrubbing and spraying they did. The coloring had lightened some but each symbol left an imprint underneath, as if they had been burned into there.

Leo growled and threw the towel at the wall. "What the hell did these people use?"

Addison collapsed onto the couch. "Forget it. I'll call a cleaning crew. We'll let the professionals handle this." Leo plopped down next to her and put his head on her shoulder. She loved it when he cuddled like this. "I was thinking you and grandma should come and stay with me. We'll give the police time to look into this and Grandma won't have to be afraid of being in this big, empty house alone."

"I love you Mom, but between your dating life and your fires, I think I'll steer clear. I'll move in here for a while. Grams will love that." He kissed her cheek to lessen the sting of his rejection.

"Moms are allowed to date, you know. And those fires are accidents." She blew out a breath. There was no changing his mind. He was as stubborn as his father.

On her way home, she'd call Fitz and Iggy and ask them to stay over too. Between the three of them, they would keep her mom distracted long enough for her to talk to Xavier and get to the bottom of this.

eight

ADDISON STOOD behind the counter at *The Addictive Bean*, counting the minutes until she could go home.

Molly, a regular of the shop, walked up tentatively. "Addison dear, I have a problem."

"Well, let's see if I can solve it for you." Addison really adored the older woman. She was the type of woman you just knew had never said an unkind word in her life and gave everything she had to help another person.

Molly leaned in. "I had taken my teeth out while I was eating a muffin." Oh no, Addison had a bad feeling. "I had put them on the tray and I guess a napkin covered them at some point because I dumped the entire tray in the garbage can."

Addison groaned inside as she smiled on the outside. "I can definitely help with that. How hard can it be?"

She grabbed a pair of gloves from under the counter and went around to the garbage can.

"Well, I emptied my tray a while ago. I was finishing my book before I left, so they may not be on top."

Of course, it wouldn't be that easy.

She opened the door of the cubby the trash can was in and pulled the almost full bin out. As she stuck her hands in it crossed her mind that she didn't get paid well enough to do this. There were so many germs from other people's mouths in there. Even with gloves on, she didn't want to touch any of it.

The can shook violently as trash flew upward and spewed several feet in every direction. People screamed as they ran to the opposite side of the store.

Callie, her manager, ran out of the back. "What now?"

Addison was mortified. One more weird thing to add to the list. She pulled a banana peel off her shoulder. "It's okay. I have everything under control."

Several people murmured as they grabbed their stuff and left.

"Oh, look." Molly cheered as she bent down and picked up her dentures. "You're a lifesaver, Addison. If you tell me where the broom is, I'll help you clean up."

Callie shook her head. "That's okay Ms. Molly. We got this."

"Well, if you're sure. I'll see everyone tomorrow." She waved at each of them and left.

Addison watched the older woman leave. She knew what was coming.

"Addison, this is getting out of control. I get some people are just clumsy, but you take it to the extreme." She grabbed a broom and swept garbage toward the can. "I don't want to let you go. I need you to be more careful, though."

Nausea rolled through Addison. This was her first real job. She didn't want to be fired from it. She had to get this chaos under control. "I'm trying. I really am. Don't give up on me yet."

Callie had been divorced for almost two years. She had taken pity on Addison and hired her, knowing full well Addison had no experience. This was not how she wanted to repay Callie's kindness.

They got the lobby clean and cleared the line of customers quickly. Callie hung the broom up and stretched her back. "I think that's enough for today. Darla has everything covered. You can head out." Darla, the newest hire, nodded from behind the cash register.

They would probably be thrilled when she was out of their way.

She clocked out and dragged herself to her car. Some people recharged with music. Not her. When she was stressed, she craved the silence. Everything would get quiet and slowly her mind would too.

She got home in record time and kicked her shoes off at the door. She still hadn't recovered from the last forty-eight hours. When she'd gotten home from her mom's the day before, she managed to get a couple of hours of sleep before going on her date and boy, was she glad she did. Andy was tall, with a dazzling smile. He was a pretty damn good kisser, too. He'd surprised her by taking her to a bowling alley. Everything had gone pretty well except for a couple of times when her ball jumped lanes, and the few minutes when all the ball return machines sucked the balls back in and shot them out by the pins. Everyone chalked it up to a mechanical malfunction. She knew that wasn't it. Somehow, it was because of her. After that, she'd crawled into bed alone and slept a few more hours before going to work where she'd made the trash can explode.

With Jerry, she hadn't had to work. In retrospect, that was probably a big reason she had become so isolated. She sure loved the paycheck, but wasn't a fan of working full time. She had to remind herself it was better than being dependent on another person to even buy a cup of coffee.

Her bed called to her, but she was going to ignore it until she looked into the symbols. It had been driving her crazy all day at work. Callie had a no phones out when customers were around policy. It was a coffeehouse. There were always customers around.

She changed into sleep shorts and a tank top, heated soup on the stove, and then settled on the couch with her laptop. With the entirety of the internet at her fingertips, surely she'd have this figured out quickly. In Google she trusted.

Screw Google. Okay fine, Google rocks. In the last four hours, she'd filled pages of a notebook with the information she'd learned. There was no smoking gun though, to explain how the symbols got in her mother's house to begin with.

Everything pointed toward witchcraft. She couldn't deny what had been happening to her sure did seem like magic, but she still didn't buy into the whole thing. One thing was for certain, those symbols were there because of her. But why?

When the sites started pointing more and more toward dark and evil magic, she had gotten freaked out enough to clear her browsing history and toss her laptop away from her.

There had been a few books that were referenced repeatedly and when she looked up where to buy them close to her, she found a quirky little shop that had recently opened in town that she hadn't had a chance yet to check out.

She grabbed her phone and dialed the shop.

"*Soul Apothecary*, Luna speaking."

"Hi. I have some symbols I'm researching and I saw you might carry some of the books I'm looking for. I wanted to see if they were in stock?"

"Oh, I'm sure I do. I love research. Bring your symbols by tomorrow and we'll look at them together." A bell could be heard in the background. "I have a customer. I'll see you in the morning."

And like that, the whirlwind that was Luna hung up. The girl talked like she had drunk five gallons of coffee.

Addison wasn't sure she wanted to share the markings with a stranger. That would mean admitting that maybe magic was real.

But her mother was scared, and that wasn't okay.

To get through this, she was going to have to keep going. Maybe it wouldn't be so bad to have someone to research with. Looking at some of that stuff alone in a dark house was not ideal. She shuddered as the images of the horned goat men sacrificing a woman came to mind.

A sneeze came out of nowhere as Addison's scalp felt like it was on fire.

She jumped up from the couch and ran to the bathroom to look in the mirror. "What the hell?"

Her normally chestnut-colored hair was now a shimmering pink. It didn't look that bad.

Another sneeze and now her hair was a deep purple. Damn, why hadn't she tried coloring her hair earlier?

Four quick sneezes and four hair color changes later, she was back to her natural color.

Stupid perimenopause. She had finally been getting into a comfortable place with her life and this crap had to start. Why couldn't she just have hot flashes like everyone else?

nine

ADDISON FELT a mix of dread and excitement as she drove to *The Soul Apothecary*. She had to hope if Luna worked in a place like that, she was open-minded enough not to think Addison was crazy. Just in case, she was going to share as little as possible.

She managed a parking spot right in front of the shop. She loved it when a store stayed on theme and this one didn't disappoint. Various occult symbols were on the windows and the displays were of crystals, sage, and what Addison had to assume was a joke, the wands from the Harry Potter series.

Gathering her courage, she went inside. The faint scent of incense tickled her nose. She was never a huge fan of those.

The soft jingle of the bell over the door alerted

the young woman behind the counter to look up from her book. "You must be the woman who called last night. You didn't tell me you were a witch."

Addison froze. Was there an invisible blinking sign over her head that only magic people could see? She forced a chuckle. "I'm definitely not a witch and I'm not sure magic even exists."

The girl snorted. "I'm Luna. This is my shop, and magic is most definitely real. Watch." She closed her eyes and took a deep breath. The hair on Addison's arms stood up from the electric feeling in the air as the girl whispered.

Crystals of all shapes and sizes rose and formed long lines that crisscrossed around the store. They danced and shimmered in the bright light of the fluorescent bulbs overhead.

It was incredible. She'd never really tried to do something on purpose. A bowl of crystals unmoving caught Addison's eye. She focused on the small objects and pictured them rising and dancing along with the others.

Excitement bubbled inside her as they started shaking in the bowl. This was it. She was going to do it.

The lights overhead flickered as the crystals that were swirling around the store turned into projectiles and pinged around the store. Most aimed for the bowl Addison had been focusing on. The sound of glass breaking behind her sent dread down her body. She had to hope there wouldn't be a fire next.

Luna screeched as a vase on a nearby shelf shattered. "Enough!" She shouted. Everything in the store stilled. One by one, the crystals flew back to their respective bowls and stopped moving.

Addison turned and met Luna's glare. "Not a witch? Your magic powers that don't exist just wreaked havoc with my spell. Don't you know not to go interfering with another witch's incantation?"

"Of course, I didn't know that. I'm not a witch." If she said it enough times, maybe someone would believe her. She did feel bad, though. The damage was likely because of her. "I feel bad. How about I buy that vase that broke? I'm sure with a little glue it will look great again."

Luna bent down behind the counter and then stomped over to the shattered crystal with a small broom and dustpan. "You're not ready for this. I can just imagine the chaos you would cause with this."

"Chaos? With a vase? I mean, I guess I could do a pretty insane flower arrangement or something."

"The fact that you don't know what this is proves you shouldn't have it." She finished cleaning up and puttered around the store as she mumbled to herself. After a couple of minutes, she walked up to Addison with a stack of books and a necklace. "You might want to start with the basics. These books will help with that. You should wear the amulet at all times. It will help protect you... mostly from yourself."

The jade stone with a large gold symbol on it hung from a thin, black braided chain. Even if it didn't hold any magical abilities, it was beautiful enough that she'd wear it anyway.

Luna handed off the large pile and went back to her stool behind the counter. "How about you show me the symbols you were researching?"

Addison opened the photo album on her phone and passed it over to Luna. "I was touring an old house and saw these. I tried looking them up online, but couldn't find these exact ones."

Luna swiped through each photo. Her face grew more serious with each one she saw. With a heavy sigh, she slid the phone back across the counter. "Now, how about the real story?" She crossed her arms and stared at Addison.

The silence echoing around the shop was deafening. Telling the truth about where the symbols came from didn't necessarily mean she was admitting to being a witch. Luna seemed knowledgeable and genuinely wanted to help.

Addison's shoulders dropped. "Fine. They showed up in my mother's living room in the middle of the night. She's not a witch, doesn't have an inkling of weirdness in her. The one camera she had didn't show anyone coming or going from the locked house. Are you satisfied with that answer?"

"Yes, because I believe you. I think you have a problem, though. Symbols like these are personal to the witch who cast them. The power is in the intent while they made these. The fact that they snuck into your mom's house makes me think they have ill intent. You are going to need a lot more than one amulet."

Addison's head fell back as she stared at the ceiling. "Well, fuck me sideways."

ten

ADDISON GRABBED the box of pastries she'd brought home from work and walked them over to Cecil's house. Theo's police car was in the driveway. She was glad to see he was checking on his grandfather more often.

The porch was surprisingly clean. Theo's doing, no doubt. She knocked on the door and waited. Theo came from around the side of the house. "Oh, hey there. We're sitting out back. Why don't you come around?"

She went through the open gate and followed him around the house. Everything was grown over, but there was lawn equipment spread around, and Theo was shirtless and covered in sweat. She knew police officers had to be in good shape, but he was ripped. Maybe he wasn't too young for her. How much younger than herself was she willing to go? This was going to take a lot more thought and if she wanted it to be unbiased, she couldn't decide while a mouthwatering morsel of a man was standing in front of her.

He grabbed his shirt off a patio chair and put it on.

Damn.

Cecil smiled and waved to her. "Addison, have you met my grandson, Theo?"

"I have. It looks like he's helping you around here?"

Cecil leaned forward and clapped Theo on the back. "He's always been a good boy."

Theo rolled his eyes and chuckled. "Would you like to sit?"

"Sure." Balancing the box in one hand, she pulled the chair back. She didn't count on it being so springy. As she sat, the chair rocked backward, sending her feet up in the air. Lucky for everyone, Theo was fast and strong. He caught her by the ankle and keep the box from tumbling to the ground. Her sneaker slid off her foot and flew upward, hitting Theo in the face.

Addison was mortified. Why was she always

such a klutz? There was no way Theo was going to find her attractive after this.

He set the box on the table and squatted in front of her. "Are you okay?"

Cecil snorted. "Addison is always fine. The girl is a human tornado."

She scowled at the old man before turning back to Theo. "I'm fine, thank you." She pushed the box toward Cecil. "I'm not sure you deserve these after that crack, but I brought you some goodies from the coffee shop."

He likely only caught every third word. That didn't stop him from excitedly opening the box and grabbing a slice of a strawberry and cream cheese danish.

Theo looked in and grabbed a cinnamon coffee cake. "These look great. You work at *The Addictive Bean*, right?"

She cocked her head to the side. Had he been investigating her? "Yep, for a few months now."

"I haven't made it in there yet, but I patrol that route a lot. I'm more of a tea man."

"That's because of my Lily. She was from England and made us drink tea every afternoon. Theo had no choice but to love it. There was no disappointing Lily." Cecil interjected fondly.

"You know, it doesn't make sense that we don't serve tea too. I'll talk to Callie on my next shift. Can I name drop you would become a regular customer if she did? Every shop would love to have a police presence, right?"

Theo chuckled as he nodded his head. "Wow, using me for my badge?" He winked at her. "I'm kidding. I would definitely stop in if there was tea."

"Then I'm on it. I'll report back when we have it for you." She pulled her cell out of her pocket and checked the time. "I've got to get going. My mom and sons are coming over for dinner and the best part is she cooked. All I have to do is eat it."

"That sounds like the dream." He got up. "Let me make sure the chair doesn't try to kill you while you get out of it." He held his hand out for her to take.

Be still her heart, a gentleman. She got to her feet safely and waved goodbye to Cecil.

Theo followed her around the side of the house. "I wanted to let you know I'm going to be spending a lot more time here and when my lease is up, I'm moving in. I can't take him from this house. It was the first house he and my grandmother bought when they got married. Every memory he has is in this place."

Addison blinked away tears. She wished her marriage had been so beautiful. "That is incredibly sweet of you and quite the sacrifice. Are you sure you want to be a full-time caregiver? No offense, but he can be a handful."

"None taken. It's not like I'm attached to my apartment and I don't have a girlfriend to worry about. Besides, I need to take the burden off all of you. It's one thing to be neighborly. It's another to tuck him into bed at two in the morning when he's rummaging around your yard." He pulled the gate open for her.

She turned back. "It'll be nice to have you around-" When he lifted one eyebrow at her, she realized how that sounded. "For the police presence and all that."

"Right. Have a good dinner."

She blushed as she crossed the street. He was too young for her, but it still felt good to flirt a little. And nice of him to flirt back.

The smile fell from her face when she saw Marilyn at the fence line watering her plants. The woman's water bill had to be insane. "Evening Marilyn."

"Hhhmpf." Marilyn stared her down as she walked up her driveway.

"Hey, the flamingo is gone. What did you do with it?" How had Addison not noticed sooner the giant thing was gone?

"I came out this morning, and it was gone. A normal one was in its place." She shrugged like that wasn't weird.

"Any news on Cleo?" The flyers were still up, but no one had called her to report seeing the obnoxious feline.

Marilyn shocked her when she burst into tears.

Shit, now she had to comfort the woman. "Hey, don't worry. We're going to find her. She knows how good she has it here. She'll be back in no time."

A blue pickup pulled into her driveway. She didn't know anyone with that vehicle.

Xavier got out and gave her a small wave. She turned back to Marilyn. "I am sorry about Cleo. We'll find her, though."

She met Xavier halfway up the driveway. "I didn't know you had a car."

"Did you think I flew everywhere?"

She rolled her eyes. "I just meant you appear on the sidewalk. I didn't really know how you were getting around."

"I parked a few houses down." He glanced at her

chest and grabbed the amulet hanging dangerously close to her breasts.

"Hey, hands."

"Sorry. Where did you get this?" At least he looked a little embarrassed for being so forward.

"A lady at the metaphysical shop gave it to me. She said it was for protection."

He pursed his lips as he studied it. "You should never take magical objects from a stranger. You have no idea what spells could be on it." He gently dropped the amulet and stepped back. "Why did she give it to you? Did something happen that you need protection?"

She sighed. It was time to be honest with him. She couldn't deny any of this any longer. "Let's go inside. I have something to show you. We don't have much time, though. My family will be here soon."

He nodded and followed her into the house. They went back to the kitchen and sat at the table. She pulled out her phone, opened the photo album of the symbols, and slid it toward him.

His face darkened with each swipe. "Was this the call you got to go to your mom's?" She nodded. "Why didn't you call me immediately?"

"I don't know you. You mysteriously showed up and started talking about me having magic. That's a lot of red flags. I wasn't just going to spill my business to you."

He slid the phone back. "Fair point. What changed?"

She blew out a breath. "I'm not saying I'm a witch, but I can't keep denying that magic is real and I'm involved in it. When it was only impacting me, I was frustrated, but fine. Now that my mom is involved, I'm not okay with it. I need answers."

"Mom, we're here," Iggy called as he walked in the front door.

Xavier hopped up. "You want me to sneak out the back?"

"No. They know something is up. I need to be honest with them." She stood up and brushed her sweaty hands on her jeans.

Iggy walked in with a big smile on his face until he saw Xavier. One by one, Leo and Fitz came in and turned very serious. Her mother looked surprised, but excited.

"Everyone, this is my friend Xavier. He's been helping me with the symbols."

One by one, each son shook hands with him.

Theresa gave him a small wave. "It's nice to meet you. Especially if you are helping get to the bottom of whatever this is."

"It's nice to meet you, too. Can I help you with that?" He reached out and let her pass off a basket. By the smell of it, that was the garlic bread.

The boys put the rest of the containers that had the lasagna, salad, and dessert on the counter. Their normal good-natured attitudes were hidden underneath a layer of unease. Sure, this was the first man they'd seen her with since the divorce, but they all knew she was on the dating apps, so they shouldn't be so surprised.

She got their attention and gave them the wide-eyed, knock it off look.

Theresa sat and crossed her arms. "Talk first, then eat. That cleaning crew you hired came today. No luck, the marks are still there. They suggested replacing all the drywall and furniture."

"That sucks, but getting to redecorate has become my hobby, so there is a silver lining." That was no consolation, but she wanted to keep her mom from getting too worried.

"I don't understand how they burned those symbols into the wall and I didn't smell anything. I'm not that deep of a sleeper."

"If I may," Xavier waited for her to give him the go ahead. There was no time like the present. She had to rip the band-aid off.

"I'm a paranormal investigator. I've seen symbols similar to that." A mixture of shock and disbelief crossed their faces. Addison understood that. It felt like they were in a movie.

He continued on. "I think this is some kind of locator spell. I don't think anyone was in your house. The caster is sloppy, though. The markings should not have stayed behind and definitely shouldn't have burned into the surface."

"Caster…" Iggy said. "Like as in a witch casting a spell? You're saying it was magic?"

Xavier nodded.

Addison's stomach rolled. In for a penny, in for a pound. "I've seen a lot these last few days. Magic is real. It took me a long time to accept it. We think all the accidents and stuff are because I have magic and it's just now revealing itself. I don't know how to control it, so everything keeps going wonky."

Her family stared at her with jaws dropped. Fitz was chewing his nails like he does when he gets anxious.

"Forget any preconceived notions you have and think back on everything that happened. When you consider magic might be involved, everything makes sense." A weight lifted from her chest. Whether or not they believed her, she'd spoken her truth.

Leo smiled. "Does that mean we might have magic too?"

Addison looked at Xavier. She had no clue how it all worked.

"You could. Magic is usually passed genetically. It's very rare to find someone like your mom who knew nothing of magic and just randomly had it one day." Xavier answered.

Addison pursed her lips as a thought came to her. "Wait, mom. You've never heard of anyone in the family with magic? Anyone on Dad's side?"

Theresa shook her head as she got up and walked over to grab the lasagna. "No. We've had some characters in the family, but magic was never mentioned."

Iggy, always the serious one, leaned forward. "Okay. Let's say magic is real and mom is a witch. What now? She's going to get seriously hurt if she doesn't get this under control." He pinned Xavier with a stare. "Are you going to teach her? Are you going to track the symbols so we can find out why they did it and what they were looking for?"

Xavier shook his head sadly. "I have no magic to speak of. It's buried deep in my family line. There hasn't been a caster for generations."

Addison studied him. He looked genuinely upset

that he wasn't a witch. It had brought her nothing but trouble so far. Maybe it would get better when she had learned some stuff. "You know that new store in town, *The Soul Apothecary,* the woman who owns it, is a witch. She gave me some books to start with. Once I get through those, I'm going to go back and see what she suggests I do next. I'm just as eager as you are to stop the chaos."

The real question was, if she learned to control her power, was that any guarantee things would get better? Or would it open a whole new can of magical worms? There was only one way to find out.

eleven

ADDISON DUG around her ever-growing laundry pile to find the cleanest, best-smelling items she could put on. She may have missed a laundry day or two in the last week. She laid a shirt and pants on the bed, grabbed the bottle of Febreze for fabric, and sprayed down the clothes. She flipped the outfit over and did it again.

If anyone asked what her perfume was, she would say lilac garden. No need to mention the Febreze part. As she bent to put on her one pink and one green sock, she noticed a stain on her pants. Was it noticeable enough to warrant going through all her clothes again? She looked at the pile and shook her head. If anyone was rude enough to comment, she didn't want to be friends with them anyway.

She'd been so excited when it became a trend to wear mismatched socks. It really made life easier. With Jerry, her house had been spotless, every article of clothing neatly put away. On her own, she was too busy living life to worry about how perfect everything was. And she loved every minute of it.

She rushed out to her car and skidded to a stop when she noticed a note tucked under her windshield wiper. Flipping it open, it was from Marilyn, and Hell must have frozen over. The woman was asking for Addison's help.

She pulled her cell phone out of her back pocket. "Shit." She was going to be late for work. Marilyn needed her, and she still felt bad about the whole cat/flamingo thing, so she texted her boss that she would be in ASAP.

Xavier's shiny blue truck pulled up to her house. The man must not have anything better to do than hang around her. Not that she minded. He was gorgeous, age-appropriate, a great dresser, and damn if he didn't always smell good. Right now though, she had to deal with Marilyn and get to work. "Morning. Not to be rude, but I don't have time to hang out right now."

He held up a book for her. "Not a problem. I was dropping this book about magic and how the moon affects it off for you to check out. You mentioned last night you had to work, so I was going to leave it by the front door. Is everything okay?"

"That sounds like a great read, thank you." She waved the note in the air. "Marilyn said she needs my help. I would have thought the woman would rather die than ask me for anything, so I'm going to see what's going on."

"Want me to come as backup in case she goes off on you and you try to hex her or something?" He smiled innocently.

She started to argue, then thought better of it. "Actually, it might be smart to have you there. She knows how to push my buttons and, like you said, in my current state, I'm dangerous."

He nodded and stepped back for her to lead the way. As they walked up the sidewalk to Marilyn's front door, she could feel the beady eyes of the plastic flamingos judging her.

As soon as they stepped onto the porch, the front door opened. Marilyn stood there with tears pouring down her face.

"What happened?"

"My... Cleo..." she gasped between each word. "She's... gone."

Addison and Xavier exchanged glances. Addison was thoroughly confused. "We already knew that."

"No!" Marilyn shook her head vigorously. "She had shown back up last night. This morning I got up to make her breakfast, and she was gone again." Her chin quivered as another sob wracked her body.

Addison didn't think she ever loved an animal that much. That thought made her sad. She'd have to look into getting a pet when everything was settled down. Not a dog or a cat, though, something cool.

Xavier patted the older woman's shoulder. "I'm sure she's not far. She obviously knows how to get back. You'll probably see her by dinnertime."

Marilyn's eyes widened. "She didn't leave me. Something took her. I saw it."

Crazy woman says what? Addison really didn't have time for this. "What do you mean you saw something take her?"

Marilyn pulled her phone out of her pocket and gave it to them. A video was paused on the screen. Addison stepped closer to Xavier and hit play. It was a view of Marilyn's living room from a security camera. Cleo walked in from the hallway and froze. Suddenly she was thrust into the air, shook around, and then disappeared into thin air.

"What the hell?" Addison had never seen anything like it in her life. Her cell phone chimed in her back pocket. She handed Marilyn's phone back to her and checked her own.

Callie texted, asking her to hurry. Bethany, one of the other baristas, had to leave, so Callie was alone and swamped.

Addison was so torn. She wanted to watch that insane cat video again, but she wouldn't let Callie down. "Listen. I have to go to work, but it's only a four-hour shift. You stay put and I'll be back as soon as I can. Okay?"

"If it's okay, I'd like to help too." Xavier offered.

Marilyn sobbed again. "Thank you both so much. I'll see you in four hours."

Addison should have padded the time a bit. Marilyn was not accounting for travel time. Thankfully, she didn't have Addison's phone number, or she'd likely start texting in exactly four hours.

Xavier walked Addison back to her car. "Drive safe to work and I'll see you in a few hours." He held her door open and closed it when she was in. Gentlemen were a dying breed.

She waved goodbye and pulled out of the drive-way. How on earth was she supposed to pour coffee and clean trash for the next four hours when she'd just seen a cat evaporate?

twelve

ADDISON WANTED nothing more than to go home after work, drink wine while she took a bath, and then pass out in the center of her king-size bed.

Unfortunately, Marilyn was waiting for her. She'd promised to help and she would follow through. Not that Marilyn had ever given Addison any reason to be helpful.

She smiled when she saw Xavier's truck out front of her house. He'd become a daily part of her life, and she didn't want to admit how much she liked it. She wasn't ready for anything but casual flings. She had some oats to sow.

She parked in her driveway and walked to the curb to meet Xavier. "So Detective, what's the plan?

I don't have any clue what to do after seeing Cleo disappear like that."

He fell in step next to her as they walked to Marilyn's. "We need to search from top to bottom and look for clues. It's rare for the paranormal to not leave some residual trace."

"This is my first investigation. Could you be a little more specific about what I'm looking for?"

"You'll know it when you see it." He gave her a cheesy smile.

She went to snap back at him but got distracted by the judgy plastic flamingos. It was like they were afraid of being turned into eight-foot monstrosities or something. Sheesh.

Marilyn had the door open before they reached the top step of the stairs. "Thank goodness. I've been going insane. I couldn't even concentrate long enough to prune my rose bushes."

Whoa. That was serious. She once saw Marilyn working in her garden during a hailstorm. Nothing stopped her.

"Ma'am, are you okay with us coming in and looking around?" Xavier asked politely.

Didn't he know Marilyn was her nemesis?

Marilyn swung the front door wide. "Absolutely. Anything to find my Cleopatra."

They turned left into the living room where the video had been taken and stopped in shock. There were pictures of Cleo everywhere. Large framed photos, small ones on the tabletops. There was even a creepy stuffed version of the cat sprawled across the top of the couch.

How did she have this much time to be obsessed with her cat when she was so focused on her garden?

Xavier pointed to a door on the far wall. "You start that way. I'll go back and check the other side of the house."

Addison nodded. She was relieved to see Marilyn didn't follow her. Down the short hallway were three doors. The first was a standard bathroom. She didn't find anything of note there except that all of Marilyn's lotions and soaps were flower-scented.

Obsessed...

The next door led to a bedroom. Or a cat room would be a better name for it. There was a tiny four-poster bed engulfed in small pillows and fur blankets. Cleopatra was painted in gold on the wall behind the bed. Even more pictures of the obnoxious cat were all over this room.

Marilyn needed help.

She swung the last door open and gasped. A small bedroom was covered in the same symbols from Addison's mom's house. Marilyn didn't think to mention these?

Addison was picking at one of the symbols, confirming they were burned into the surface like Theresa's were when Xavier rushed into the room.

"Look at this." He held up a large leather book with similar symbols on them. "I found this in her craft room. I've never actually met anyone with an entire room in their house dedicated to crafting."

Addison squinted at him. "Xavier... focus."

"Sorry-" He paused when he finally noticed the markings. "I told you would know when you saw it."

Addison shook her head at him. "What about the book? Does the book decode the symbols?"

"No, but there is something else important about it." He set the book on the bed and opened it. It was in a language she didn't understand, but her name was repeatedly listed.

"What the hell?" She dropped to her knees and flipped page after page. Her name was there, clear as day. "Can you read this?"

"I've gotten decent at Latin but this is Gaelic. It's going to take some time, but we'll translate it."

She snatched the book up and went to find Marilyn. She found the older woman sitting at her kitchen table, staring at a photo of Cleo.

Addison slammed the book down. "What is this? Why is my name in it? And why do you have it?"

Marilyn stared at it wide-eyed. "I have no idea. I've never seen that before."

Xavier sat in a chair next to her. "I found it wrapped in a cloth in the vent of your craft room."

Both women snapped their heads toward him.

"Damn, you are thorough," Addison said. She didn't know she was supposed to be checking vents. Was she supposed to be looking for false walls and floorboards that lifted to reveal small storage areas? Day one as a paranormal detective and she already sucked at it.

"I swear, I have no idea how that got there." Marilyn pleaded. She glanced down at the book. "Why would I want a book that talks about your family history and prophecies?"

Xavier and Addison glanced at each other.

Addison pointed to a page. "You can read this? You can read Gaelic?"

Marilyn glanced down and studied it. "I don't think I can. I don't know why I would." She picked it up and scanned each line. "I can pick up a word here and there, but it's like I used to know the language but can't remember it anymore."

"Do you mind if we take this?" Xavier asked.

"Of course. I have no use for it and if it has her name in it, it must be hers." That was surprisingly logical for Marilyn. "What does any of this have to do with my Cleo, though?"

"I'm not sure." He looked right at Addison. "You're not going to like this. I think Marilyn is connected to you."

Addison grimaced. That was exactly what she didn't want to hear. "You're probably right. I think we should take the book to Luna and see if she can tell us anything."

Marilyn stood up. "I don't know who this Luna is, but if she can help find my Cleo, I'm going with you."

Addison's shoulders dropped. How was she going to be able to talk freely in front of Marilyn? If she hadn't thought Addison was weird before, she was about to get a whole lot more ammunition. Within days, the entire neighborhood would know Addison thought magic was real, and she was a witch. Soon people would whisper she's the scary witch whose house you crossed the street to avoid.

Addison blew out a breath. She had to shut her

mind down before she spiraled. She had to focus on deciphering the symbols and finding the cat that vanished into thin air. Just another day in the chronicles of Addison Schmidt.

THE NEWLY FORMED and very odd trio drove to Luna's shop in Xavier's truck. Marilyn's eyes were still red-rimmed, but at least she had stopped crying.

Luna was cashing out a teenager buying a bunch of sage. She must have a serious ghost problem if she was buying that much.

Addison was proud of herself. She'd spent every free minute reading the books from Luna and sage was one of the first things she'd learned about. Not that she was totally sure yet that ghosts, vampires, and all the other supernatural stuff she read about were real. If so, where were they all?

Luna gave Xavier a slow once-over. When Addison had done it, she was appreciating his looks and body. Luna looked like she was sizing him up. "He reeks of the supernatural, but I don't think he is anything special."

Ouch. There was probably a nicer way she could have said that. By Xavier's scowl, he felt the same.

When the shopkeeper glanced over at Marilyn, she did a double take. She rushed around the counter and circled Marilyn as she poked and pulled at something invisible. "This is incredible."

"Hello. I'm Addison's neighbor, Marilyn. She said you can help me find my cat."

Luna turned her head one way and then the other. What on earth was she doing?

Addison cleared her throat loudly. "Is everything okay?"

"First of all, she's magical. I'm not sure I'd say a witch. I read auras and there is something really off with hers. It's almost solid black. I've never seen anything like it. This is going to take some research."

Marilyn had magic? What the hell?

"Speaking of research," Addison held up the book. "We found this in her house. She claims she has no knowledge of what it is or how it got in her house."

Luna's eyes lit up. She waved them to a table in the back corner and pulled out chairs for everyone.

Addison and Xavier sat while Marilyn walked around and looked at everything. She had already grabbed a basket and was filling it with stuff. If the woman was magical, she sure acted like everything in that store was brand new to her. She held up a basket of dried snake skins. "What a collection." She set them down and raced over to a shelf filled with the eyeballs of different animals. Addison hated that shelf. It always gave her the willies. Marilyn looked like a kid on Christmas.

Luna flipped through the book, her fingers gently sliding down each page as if she were reading Braille. When she got to the end, she closed it gently and sat back. "Fascinating."

Addison sat forward excitedly. "So you can read it? What does it say about me?"

"Haven't a clue. We'll have to translate it."

Xavier snorted. "Gee. Why didn't I think of that? Oh, wait, because I'm not special."

Luna nodded as if she agreed.

Addison took a deep breath. These two were going to be the death of her.

Luna held up her finger to have them stay put and came back with her laptop. "I believe it's your family's spell book. It goes back centuries. The history of your ancestors must be incredible."

Addison shook her head in frustration. "My family is not magical. There is some mistake."

Luna ignored her and went back and forth between the book and the computer. After a painfully long time, she turned the computer. "Here's the first page."

The Grimoire of Addison Schmidt and all those who came before her.

Every female in the Schmidt lineage is born with immense power that connects us to the previous generations. There is power in a name, so all females are passed down the name Addison after the very first Schmidt witch. Use the magic in this book carefully. You have the power to end the world at your fingertips. You must take care at all times to control your power and protect this book from those who seek to harm.

It went on to list Addison's with date ranges. The last line had her birth year but no end year. Could that be her entry? "This makes no sense. My mom's name is Theresa."

Xavier reached over and squeezed her hand that she had balled into a fist. "I think you need to have a conversation with your mom. Something is going on that she isn't telling you."

Addison felt sick to her stomach. Why did every day seem to get a little worse instead of better? Did she want to hear whatever her mom would tell her?

Marilyn walked up and held her hand up. "Is it time to talk about my Cleo now?"

Luna waved to the empty chair next to her. "Tell me everything."

Marilyn went on to talk about the giant flamingo, Cleo disappearing, reappearing, and then disappearing again. She showed her the video of Cleo vanishing.

Luna clucked her tongue for a few seconds. "Between the three of us, sorry normie, I think we have enough power we can do a summoning spell. Let's call to Cleo and find out from her what is happening."

Addison and Marilyn were stunned, while Xavier looked pissed. "I'd rather be a normie than a snobby witch."

Addison rolled her eyes and ignored their little pissing contest. "I don't understand. The cat's not dead. How do you summon something that isn't dead?" Add that to the list of things that made little sense to Addison.

Luna walked around the shop, grabbing items. "Magical creatures can be summoned too. If the cat is that important to Marilyn, who is magical, it's likely the cat is too."

The bell over the door rang at the worst time. Addison wanted answers.

"I'll get rid of them quickly." Luna whispered as she got up to greet the young couple.

The tension around them continued to build as they waited for Luna to finish. Addison heard them mention something about a baby.

Luna sold them some tea leaves and a bottle of something and ushered them out the door. She flipped the sign on the door to closed and came back with several small candles which she set around the table. She shoved the laptop and grimoire in front of Xavier and laid several stones with ruins on them around the table in a circle. "Do you have anything of Cleo's with you?"

Marilyn nodded as she dug into her purse. "Here, this is her special occasion collar." The royal purple leather had dime-sized jewels every few inches and gold stitching.

Crazy. That was all Addison could say about her

neighbor. Not that she was jealous of a cat or anything, but she was pretty sure she didn't own anything that nice.

Luna held out her hands. Addison was scared to grab it. Shit was getting real. Was she ready for that? The book said she was super powerful. Would she blow up the shop with them in it?

"Addison, I promise you got this. As long as you stay in the circle-" She pointed at a line painted on the ground that Addison hadn't noticed before. "Everything will be fine. I'll break contact if anything goes wrong." Luna assured her.

The only way to get answers was to keep going. Addison's hand shook as she clasped Luna's and then Marilyn's.

Luna took a deep breath and closed her eyes. Everyone jumped when the candles lit without being touched. "We three summon the cat, Cleo. Your owner is here. Come to us. We three summon thee." She chanted the last line a few more times. Several forms of people and other animals appeared. Luna told them one by one to leave until she blew out a breath in frustration. "Addison, you are pushing out chaotic waves of power. Are you picturing Cleo in your head?"

Oops. Was she supposed to be doing that? She

shrugged and tried to look innocent. "Well, not exactly. You didn't tell me to." Marilyn gave her a disgusted look. Like she knew that's what they were supposed to do. "Sorry. Geez, I'll focus."

Luna repeated the summoning. Almost immediately, a ghostly apparition of Cleopatra appeared in the center of the table. "It's about fecking time. It took you long enough to get your head out of your ass and figure this shite out." She licked her paw while the rest of them processed the gravelly male voice with a distinctly Scottish brogue coming from the cat. "And what's this owner shite? She's my wife."

All eyes snapped to Marilyn, who looked ready to pass out. "Why is my cat talking? Why does it sound like a man? And why does it say I'm its wife?"

With each question, her voice got higher.

Addison cleared her throat. "Cleo, could you slow down? We're a little confused."

The cat glared at her. "You're telling me. I've been trying to talk to you for months. I was so excited when a witch moved in next door. I thought all our problems were solved, but no, you were clueless."

"All that yowling at my window was you trying to talk to me?" More than once, she'd wanted to harm the cat when it wouldn't shut up. Now she finds out it was him asking for help. "You're obviously not a female cat named Cleopatra. Are you in trouble, or did you disappear on purpose?"

"My name is Antony. When my wife, Norma, was spelled into losing her memory and magic, I was cursed into this form. It was a cruel joke to make me a female, but the pampering was nice."

Luna gasped. "Cleopatra like Marc Antony and Marilyn like Norma Jean. It's crazy how the brain works."

"Yeah, I guess that's how Norma came up with these names." The cat turned and looked at Marilyn — no, Norma. "I love you, lass, but you need to snap out of this. For some reason, I was able to remember our names, and that you were magical. Everything else is a blur. I need you back so you can fix me."

Antony snapped his head around, watching for something behind him. "I don't have much time. I'm being held by a couple of witches. They keep kidnapping me. Somehow, they know I'm a man trapped in this form. They want some book, and they keep mentioning Addison's name and taking her powers." He glanced behind him again. "Shit, they're coming. I love you, honey, now come find me."

The cat disappeared as the candles went out.

Luna fell back against her chair. "Woah, that was heavy."

Xavier handed the book to Addison. "Well, now we know you guys are definitely connected, and it has to do with this book. You need to talk to your mom."

Marilyn squealed. "No. You need to help me rescue Cleo, I mean Antony. I have no idea what is happening and I'm pretty sure this is all a dream, but he sounded scared. Please, you have to help me."

Addison glanced at a clock on the wall. She was supposed to have a date in a couple of hours. She had already shaved and everything. Marilyn's pleading eyes swam with unshed tears.

"Fine." Why go out with a hot man when she could play special ops and rescue a man trapped as a cat being held by witches hunting her?

fourteen

WHERE DID THEY EVEN BEGIN? Addison turned to Xavier. "You're a supernatural investigator. It feels like this might be more your territory. What do we do?"

Luna laughed loudly. "Ah, so you're a groupie."

He scowled at her. "I'm not a groupie. My family is magic. I just don't have any. You think you're so much better than me? Why don't you come up with the plan?"

They went back and forth, throwing out ideas while arguing about why the other's plan wouldn't work. Addison regretted ever introducing those two to each other.

"I could do a spell to locate every magical person

in town. We can go one by one and rule them out." Luna offered.

Xavier shook his head. "I was here ten minutes and realized how inundated this town is with the supernatural. It will take days, if not weeks, to vet everyone. Why don't we get a werewolf shifter to catch Cleo's sent and track him?"

Luna snorted. "Do you know a werewolf shifter? I certainly haven't met any yet. I'm not sure our first meeting with the local pack should be asking for their help."

Marilyn cleared her throat. "If I may, I might know where he is. Since his disappearance, I've been having dreams about a warehouse. I could see a partial sign on the door that said *Sunbeam Ent.* The dream played on repeat while I slept, to the point it was driving me insane. I searched and found Sunbeam Enterprises across town. I drove by one day but the place looked abandoned. I really didn't think my cat was being held hostage inside, so I went home and tried to forget about it. Now that I've seen all this craziness, I'm thinking that is exactly where he's being held."

"Well, that makes things easy," Xavier said, as he pulled up his GPS and typed the business in. "It's ten minutes from here. Let's go."

Addison's eyes bulged. "I'm sorry. Did you hear the part about witches holding him? We can't just walk in and take him."

Luna got up and walked behind the counter. "I have a few things that can even the odds."

"You don't know any other witches that could come and help?" Xavier asked.

She sniffed. "I've only been here a couple of months. I've been busy with the shop. I haven't had time to meet people yet."

She stuffed a few small vials in her pockets and then handed Xavier and Marilyn each an amulet. "These won't protect against everything, but will hopefully keep you from dying."

"Comforting," Xavier said dryly.

Addison grabbed the grimoire and waited as Marilyn bought the items from her basket because that made sense to do right at this moment. Luna ran Marilyn's card and leaned forward. "It's declining. Do you have another?"

Marilyn took out cash and coins and counted it slowly. Who even carried cash anymore? She grabbed her bag of goodies and turned around with a satisfied smile. She stopped when she saw Addison scowling at her. "What?"

"If you're done with your little shopping excursion, maybe we can go rescue your cat husband now?"

The older woman huffed. "Yes, yes. I'm coming. Your generation is so impatient."

"What are you even going to do with that stuff?" If she didn't know anything about magic, the ingredients she bought wouldn't be of much use.

Marilyn's mouth opened and closed a couple of times. "Well, I don't know. I feel like I need this stuff, though."

Luna shut the lights off. "Okay, you two, let's go." She locked up the shop, and the foursome drove in Xavier's truck to the warehouse. It was derelict and vacant, like Marilyn had said. Addison wouldn't have thought to look for the cat in there, either.

They parked a street over and crept between the buildings. Luna pointed at the building. With its walls missing chunks of drywall and the metal roof covered in rust, it looked like it would collapse at any minute. "Addison take a deep breath. Clear your mind and open your senses. What do you feel?"

Excitement coursed through her. This was her first lesson in magic. At first, there was nothing. No lights, or energies, or big arrows saying 'witch here'. As she cleared her mind of expectations, things quickly happened. "Oh wow. I can feel two balls of energy to the right in the building. I don't sense a third one."

Luna smiled proudly. "Excellent. I sense the same. Those balls are their energy signatures. Can you tell if there's anything odd about the actual building? Maybe a haze, or electric current?"

Addison focused again and strained her eyes, thinking that would help. "No. I don't see anything."

"That's okay. You'll get there. I can see a light blue glow around the building. I think it's just a perimeter alarm, not something that will hurt us," Luna replied.

"It takes away our element of surprise, though. You don't know how to get around it?" Xavier asked from behind them.

Luna rolled her eyes. "Witches don't know every spell in the world and how to counteract them."

"Lucky for you, I'm here." He winked at Addison and took off.

"Shit. He's going cowboy," Luna growled and took off after him.

They caught up and watched as he pulled a weird set of goggles out of his jacket pocket and put them on. They made his eyes look twice their normal size. He grabbed a crystal prism-like object from another pocket and set it on the ground. He slowly slid it forward a centimeter at a time.

After a few seconds, Luna clapped her hands. "Okay normie, I'll give you props for that."

Addison squinted her eyes. "What am I missing?"

"The object is deflecting the magic without setting it off. It's created a small bubble we can crawl through." She replied.

Xavier stood up and brushed his knees off. "I'll put one hand where the top is and one where the left side is. Since Luna can see the glow too, she can put her hand on the other side. It's very important you guys make yourselves small and don't touch our hands or you'll push them into the alarm. Got it?"

He looked ridiculous with his extra big eyes staring down at her. She stifled a laugh. "Got it."

Luna and Xavier got into position. Addison went first so she could open the door on the other side and Marilyn could get through.

"I really wished I had dressed better for this." Crawling in flip-flops was not ideal. Thankfully, she was still in her work clothes, so she didn't mind if they got dirty. But when she got off shift, she always changed shoes before she even got out of the parking lot. Her feet had serious claustrophobia about being in closed-toe shoes.

She held her breath as she slowly shuffled forward. Even though she couldn't see anything, she certainly felt some kind of power as she passed through the barrier. She contorted enough to reach up and touch the door handle. The witches' egos must be big. They hadn't bothered to lock it.

The door swung open quietly. She slipped inside and held her hand out to help Marilyn through.

Luna came next, followed by Xavier. Somehow he managed to not have a single wrinkle on his suit and his hat had never moved. Classy.

As their eyes adjusted to the dark, they could see it was one giant room with scattered tables and broken machines. There were four doors along the right wall.

The second door from the end was where the two witches were. They'd split up to check the other three doors. With any luck, Antony would be in one of them and they could rescue him and get him out without anyone knowing.

Addison took the first door. It opened without a sound. She used her phone flashlight to check and see the room was bare except for a few empty shelves lining the walls. No kitties being kept prisoner.

Luna and Marilyn walked out of the second door and shook their heads.

Xavier dashed out of the last room, holding Antony in the air. He looked so proud of himself. They raced over to him. Marilyn grabbed the cat and squished it to her chest. Now that Addison knew that was her husband, she figured the cat was probably enjoying that.

"Okay. Let's get out of here."

A low growl froze them in place. Several pairs of yellow eyes glowed around the room.

Addison groaned. "This can't be good. Any chance witch's eyes glow like that?"

Luna and Xavier shook their heads.

"I can smell them. Those are shifters." Antony said.

It was still jolting to hear the man's deep voice come from the tiny feline.

"On three, we run," Xavier whispered.

Addison tensed, ready to take off.

Xavier hadn't even said one when all hell broke loose.

Several growls came from around the room as large bears, wolves, and even a badger took off toward them. The door the witches were in swung open. Their group was trapped.

Addison yelled, "Lights on." So they could at least see to flee.

Marilyn and Luna took off toward the backdoor while Xavier and Addison ran toward the door they'd come in. Luna pulled one of the vials out of her pocket and threw it at the witches. They froze in a blob of pink goo.

Xavier was pinned against a table as a brown bear stalked him. Addison focused her attention on the machines. "On." All at once, metal screeching and whirring sounds drowned out the growls. Between Addison's wonky magic and the fact that the machines were broken, to begin with, they came alive and started attacking. Now, instead of just shifters and witches to fight, they also had machines coming after them. Oops.

A wolf howled as a machine stabbed it through the shoulder, pinning it to the wall.

Shit. That didn't look good. There goes any chance of befriending the local pack. "Sorry," she yelled toward the wolf. Shifters hadn't come up in her reading yet, so she didn't know if it could hear and understand her.

The badger came out of nowhere and jumped off

the top of a machine, landing on Addison's back. They fell to the ground. The badger got one swipe with its nails across her shoulder before Xavier was there and kicked it off of her. He helped her off the floor and together they ran for the door.

They were almost home free when the door swung open, and a woman stood there smiling at them. This must be the third witch. "Well, Addison Schmidt, the hot mess in the flesh. You're not very impressive, given your namesake."

Addison was trying to focus on the woman, but the searing pain in her shoulder and the blood running down her arm were very distracting.

"It took us a while to find you. We thought we'd find the grimoire in your place and you gave us plenty of opportunities to check thanks to all your calls to the fire department." Her looks shifted to the female firefighter who had given her a blanket during the last fire. She shifted back to herself. "We dug around in your brain but stopped when Giselle, who was watching you, saw it was causing you blinding pain in your head. You'd be no good to us incapacitated. We knew we had to be close, so we tried the locator spell again and your mother's house lit up like Christmas. You can tell her sorry for us. We had to put a lot of juice into the spell to get through the book's masking spells. We didn't mean for the symbols to remain." She shrugged and then scowled when she saw the other two witches still stuck in the pink goo. She waved her hand as she said something and the goo disappeared. They ran over and grabbed Luna and Marilyn, who'd been pinned in a corner by a set of wolves.

"Once your 'mom' and your brat son were gone, we ransacked your mom's place, but no book. We did the spell again and your neighbor's house lit up. Things were really getting interesting now. We weren't sure how they were connected. Once we realized the cat was cursed, it was a matter of getting him to tell us where the book was. He's been useless so far in that regard. We were going to search the house the next time it was empty. You beat us to it, though. Now we're going to kill you all, go to that little witch's shop, get the book, and burn the store down."

Antony yowled as the witch pulled him out of Marilyn's arms. She opened her mouth to cast a spell when Marilyn screamed. The lights went out, the building shook, and lightning bolts shot down, striking at the shifters and witches.

Xavier didn't wait around. He yanked Addison toward the door. The witch that had been monologuing was running through the parking lot as bolts rained down around her.

They made it back to the truck. Luna, Marilyn, and Antony were hot on their heels. Luna had blood covering most of her face. Marilyn was pale and shaking, but otherwise unharmed.

They jumped in the truck as Xavier peeled out of the parking lot. "What the hell was that?" Xavier asked as he sped through the streets.

Luna had ripped a piece of her shirt off and was holding it against her head. "That was Marilyn. Her magic may have been blocked, but seeing Antony about to be killed must have woken something in her."

Addison was impressed. Would she be able to shoot lightning bolts, too?

Red and blue lights blinded them.

"Fuck." Xavier cursed as he pulled over. "How are we going to explain this?"

The officer knocked on the window. "Sir, do you know why I pulled you over?"

Addison gasped. She recognized that voice. She leaned over. "Theo, hey. Sorry about that. Xavier got a little excited and wasn't paying attention to the odometer." She gave him her brightest smile.

He turned his flashlight on her, then to the

passengers in the backseat. A second later, he unholstered his gun and pointed it at Xavier. "Get out of the car now."

Xavier opened the door and held his hands up as he was shoved against the car. Theo had him handcuffed in seconds and radioed in. "I need backup. I have a male in his forties and three injured women who need ambulances."

Luna jumped out of the car and grabbed Theo's shoulder. "Nothing is wrong. It was all a misunderstanding. You'll let us go and forget you ever saw us."

Theo's face went blank. "Sorry for the misunderstanding. You can go." He took the handcuffs off Xavier and went back to his car.

Luna grabbed Xavier and shoved him toward the driver's door. "We need to go now. We have about twenty seconds before his mind clears and we don't want to be around when it does."

Xavier turned the next corner and drove the speed limit back to Luna's shop.

Addison turned in her seat. "That was insane. Can you teach me how to do that?"

Luna's face darkened. "I consider that dark magic. It can be used for terrible purposes. I wouldn't teach it to anyone. I've only used it one other time, so I'm not even sure how effective it will be."

The weight of her words settled like a pit in Addison's stomach. Dark magic was something she wanted nothing to do with.

She nodded and turned back around. In the silence, she replayed everything the witch had said. When she had said Addison's mom in air quotes, it was terrifying. Why was everyone insinuating Theresa wasn't her mother? As soon as she got everyone settled and bandaged up, she was going to take the grimoire and have a really difficult conversation with her mother. She may not want the truth, but she didn't have a choice. She had to protect her family and could only do that if she knew who and what she was.

fifteen

THEY MADE it to Marilyn's house and rushed inside. Now that they knew the witches were watching them, it felt like the darkness was hiding danger.

Marilyn grabbed her first aid kit from under the bathroom sink while Xavier filled the kitchen sink with water. She handed him a pile of towels and dragged a chair over. "It looks like Luna's head has stopped bleeding. Let's look at Addison first."

Xavier pulled a pair of scissors out of the kit. "The shirt is pretty much gone already. Is it okay if I cut the rest off? It will be less painful for you that way."

"Slice away." The less she had to move, the better.

Addison was surprised to see Marilyn right next to Xavier helping every step of the way. Luna handed her a towel to hold in front of her when they cut the bra off. That damn badger had shredded her most comfortable bra. The one that wasn't sexy, but held the girls up without hurting your back. She would have liked for Xavier's first time seeing her under clothes and they would be matching and sexy, not sturdy and full coverage. At least he seemed so focused on her injuries that he wasn't paying much attention to anything else.

"It doesn't look like you need stitches. We're going to put Steri-Strips on them to help keep them closed." Xavier spoke softly as he gently washed away the blood.

It burned like fire. She wasn't going to be the weak one, though. She gritted her teeth and let tears silently roll down her face. When they were finally done, Marilyn got a t-shirt from her bedroom and gave it to Addison to put on.

Who was this considerate woman?

Luna went next. Once they pulled the cloth away, the bleeding started up again. "You're going to need stitches. I'm not great at them. We can take you to the hospital if you prefer?" Xavier asked.

Marilyn tsked. "My sewing is impeccable. I can do it."

Sewing cloth was much different from sewing scalp. Addison was surprised when Luna agreed to let Marilyn do it. If it were her head, she'd want a professional.

It only took three stitches to close the gash. Luna hadn't made a peep.

They finished cleaning up and sat on the couch. Antony walked in and curled up on Marilyn's lap.

For a few minutes, everyone sat quietly. The adrenaline was starting to subside.

Marilyn wiped a tear from her cheek. "I want to thank you all for what you've done tonight. I still don't understand what is happening, but you risked your lives for me and my husband. That still seems weird to say. If you all need anything, don't hesitate to ask. Addison, if you want to stay here tonight so you aren't alone, that's okay, too."

Addison's jaw dropped. "That is very nice of you, but I think I'll be okay."

"Before we go," Luna interjected. "I think the three of us should cast a spell of protection over the house. That should keep the witches from entering again, physically or magically, while we figure out how to change Antony back to a human."

Marilyn set Antony aside. "If you say I will be helpful, I'm happy to try."

"First thing we need is salt." Luna hopped up and went to the kitchen. Marilyn followed to help her.

Addison glanced over to the rumpled yet still sexy Xavier. "Thank you for all of this. I'm sure this is way more than you expected when you came to town."

He chuckled. "I'm an investigator. The first rule is to have zero expectations. I will always help those in need, whether they be human or magic. I'm sticking this out with you guys as long as you want me around."

This man was dangerous to her heart. She wanted to be single and mingle. He needed to stay at arm's length.

Luna and Marilyn came back in with their hands full.

"Can you guys move the coffee table?" Marilyn asked Addison.

Xavier hopped up and lifted it by himself. Addison resisted fanning herself.

Damn, she really needed to get laid.

Luna poured a circle with the salt and laid four candles out. Marilyn handed her a bottle of garlic salt. "You said you needed salt. I thought maybe this would help keep vampires away, too."

Addison had to give Luna credit. She didn't even crack a smile. "Very thoughtful. Now why don't you and Addison sit in the circle with me?"

Addison kicked off her flip-flops that had somehow managed to stay on her feet during their run for their lives and sat where Luna pointed.

"I'm going to call to the elements. I want you to clear your minds of everything except wanting protection for this home and those inside it."

Addison didn't want to screw up like she did during the summoning, so she pictured the word *protection* in her mind and chanted it over and over again. She tuned Luna out so she wouldn't distract her. Sometimes it was rough having a mind that never shut off.

A tingle ran over Addison's body from her head to her toes. Outside sounds muffled as the scent of clover permeated the air.

Luna took a deep breath and smiled. "The spell is complete. Great job ladies."

Xavier reached down and cupped Addison's uninjured arm. "Let me help. It might be easier than putting any pressure on your injured arm."

"Thanks." He lifted her like she was light as a feather, which she most definitely was not.

Addison held her hand out to Marilyn. "Give me your phone and I'll put my number in. Call me if anything strange happens or if you see the witches lurking outside."

Phones passed around while everyone exchanged numbers. Like it or not, they were a team now.

Luna, Xavier, and Addison made their way out to the front porch and stopped when they found Cecil sitting on Marilyn's porch swing.

"Ugh, not again." Addison sighed. They needed to put a bell on the man, probably a GPS tracker too. "I'll take him home. Can you take Luna back to her shop?"

"You sure you don't want help getting him home?" Xavier asked.

"It's okay. I don't need both arms for this. He'll walk fine." She went and sat next to Cecil as Xavier and Luna left. "Cecil, this isn't your porch. You live across the street." She pointed at his house. "Come on, let's get you home."

Cecil got up effortlessly. "The supernaturals will be back. They always come back."

Addison stopped mid-step. "What did you say?"

Cecil continued down the sidewalk.

She jogged to catch up to him. "Cecil. What are you talking about?"

"They keep going in your houses. You ladies need to be more careful."

Addison was floored. So Cecil hadn't been wandering. He was keeping an eye on them. "How do you know about the supernaturals?"

Theo pulled up as they were crossing the yard. "Oh no. He left again?"

Addison shook her head. "We were having a visit, that's all. How was your shift?" Did he remember anything from the traffic stop or did Luna's spell hold strong?

He quirked his head and studied her for a second. "Did I see you earlier... no, that's not right." He shook his head to clear it. "Sorry, it's been a weird night. Dispatch swears I called in asking for backup to a traffic stop, so imagine everyone's confusion when four of my deputies converged on me."

Poor guy. She felt a little bad about causing him confusion. It was necessary though, to keep Xavier from going to jail or them having to try to explain they were witches that got hurt in a battle royale with other witches and humans that turned into animals.

That would go over well, as they put them all under a three-day psych evaluation.

sixteen

ADDISON STRETCHED awake and promptly howled in pain. She'd forgotten about her shoulder being sliced up. How was she going to hide that from her family?

She shuffled to the kitchen to nuke her instant coffee. There was no point in buying a new coffee maker until all the drama had passed. Why keep wasting money?

While that cooked, she slipped on her sneakers and went to get the mail. She was lucky if she remembered to do that every few days.

The mailbox was stuffed. Guess it had been more than a few days.

Out of the corner of her eye, she noticed Xavier's blue truck parked out front of Marilyn's house. He was sitting in the driver's seat with his hat pulled low over his eyes. She knocked on the window, causing him to jump. "Sorry. I didn't mean to scare you. What are you doing out here?"

He got out of the car and stretched. He was still in his rumpled suit. "I was worried about you guys, so I thought I'd camp out here in case anything happened."

"Oh geez. You should have told me you were coming back. You could have slept on my couch. I think we're at the point where I can trust you will not hurt me. Plus, with my awakening magic, I'd probably fry you if you tried."

His eyes bulged. "Wow, bloodthirsty. I didn't want to make anyone uncomfortable."

"Well, do you want to come in for some unquestionably gross microwaved coffee?"

His mouth turned down. "Not that that doesn't sound appetizing, but I'm going to head back to my hotel, shower, and change clothes."

"Okay. I guess I'll see you later." She walked backward as she waved and missed the curb. She fell back on her ass, the mail scattering.

She wanted to lie there and die. Or at least hide until he was gone.

If having Xavier rush to help her wasn't embarrassing enough, Theo had been going to his car, and he came over to help too.

Xavier was careful to help her up without making it obvious she had an injury hidden by her clothes while Theo collected the mail.

Xavier held her steady while Theo handed her the stack of letters. She glanced from one man to the other. Couldn't she have fallen in front of anyone else? "Thank you, both of you. I'm so embarrassed."

"It wasn't a big deal," Xavier said.

"I can trip and fall too, if that will make you feel better?" Theo asked.

"I'll help. I can push him over." Xavier smiled. Deep down, she didn't think he was joking. Maybe that was wishful thinking on her part.

"Thank you both. I'm going to take my bruised behind and battered ego and go take a shower." She grabbed the mail and tried to walk as gracefully to her door as she could. It wasn't easy knowing both men were watching her. She may have even tossed in a little hip swaying to give them something to look at. It was either sexy or made it look like she was having a stroke.

She grabbed her coffee and sat to sort the mail. A thick, black envelope made of parchment caught her eye. Her name and address were written with calligraphy, and there was no return address.

How intriguing.

She flipped it over, shocked to find it was closed with a wax seal. As gently as she could, she opened the letter and pulled out a card made of the same parchment and with the same calligraphy.

"What the what?" It was an invitation to join a secret society of supernatural beings. Were those really a thing? Or was it a trap by the witches currently making her life miserable?

Rather than risk it, she tossed it in the garbage and went back to sorting the rest of the mail.

She kept looking over at the can. The invitation sat on top, beckoning to her. She snatched it out of the garbage. "Okay. Let's think this through." She grabbed a pen and pad of paper. Across the top, she wrote *Pros* and *Cons*.

"Pros, I've never been part of a secret society before. I could make all kinds of new friends which I have been wanting since being single. I'd have more time to spend with both Xavier and Theo. Best of all, I could learn more about magic."

"Cons, People might not like me. I'm a hot mess right now. It could be a trap and I could be killed.

Xavier and Theo might not want to spend time with me."

While she contemplated her choices, there was a knock on the front door, followed by Iggy's voice. "Mom?"

"In the kitchen," she yelled back.

He walked in and kissed her cheek. "Morning. It's nice to see the house smoke-free for once."

"Haha. Smart Ass. What brings you over besides harassing me?"

His cheeks pinkened. "I've been seeing this girl, Serenity, and she asked to come over and bake cookies with me so we can bring them to a party we're going to. The problem is, I don't even own that flat plan you use when you make them."

Addison snort-laughed and then stopped. "You mean the cookie sheet? That isn't really its name either. It's called a sheet pan. Go figure." She got up and pulled the pan out of the oven where she kept all her pans. "Do you have a scoop or silicone mat?"

"I don't know what any of that is." He looked overwhelmed.

"I've failed you as a mother, and I'm sorry for that. Sometime soon we should have a big baking party here. I'll show you and your brothers all kinds of things."

Iggy's eyes widened. "That's okay. No one wants you near a kitchen right now."

She handed him the kitchen tools and sat back down at the table. "Such a smart ass."

As he was leaving, he spotted the invitation. "Secret society, what's all that about?" He set the baking items down to grab the card. "You're going to go, right?"

Addison bit her lip as she stared at the pro/con list. "I don't know. Some stuff went down yesterday and I'm worried this is a ruse."

He lifted an eyebrow. "It seems like a pretty elaborate trick if so." He sat down and grabbed her hand. "You left Dad so you could start living life. So far you've been surviving, and barely at that. If all this magic stuff is real, you need to meet other people like you. Maybe they can help stop whatever crap is causing all your fires." He stood back up. "You never know, there could be cute witches there you can set Fitz and Leo up with."

He picked up the kitchen stuff. "I'll bring this back as soon as I can."

"Feel free to bring Serenity with you." She called back.

She heard his laughter as he left. She wasn't that embarrassing, was she?

In the silence of the house, she stared at the invitation. Thanks to her laziness about checking the mail, the meeting was in a few hours. She still needed to take the Grimoire over to her mother. There had to be some mistake. There was no way she wasn't Addison's mom and there was no way if she was secretly a witch named Addison that she'd be able to keep something like that secret for this long.

No matter the outcome, she would always be her mother. Tears filled her eyes. This was going to be the scariest conversation of her life. She had no choice. She needed to know if she was the real Addison Schmidt.

seventeen

ADDISON SMOOTHED out the wrinkled sundress that had been in her dryer for the last five days, waiting to be put away. As she got to her car, she heard Marilyn call her name.

The suddenly friendly neighbor had a bag in her hand and was rushing over to the fence. "Addison, wait, I have something for you."

Addison set the grimoire on the passenger seat and joined her at the fence. "Did I forget something at your house last night?"

"Nope. I made you something." She held up the bag proudly. "Antony says that he remembers something about me being a nature witch or something. It explains why I'm so good with flowers. Anyway, I was doing some research on the Google and found a recipe for a healing poultice. It says you keep it on your wound for a couple of hours and it should rapidly speed up healing."

Marilyn looked weird with a smile on her face. Addison wasn't used to it. It kind of gave her the creeps. The woman was trying to be nice, though.

Addison opened the bag. A putrid smell burned her nose, and she gagged. "Um, wow, that's potent."

Marilyn made a stink face. "Yes, I struggled while making it. If you aren't going to use it right away, I'd keep it in the fridge or that thing might grow legs and take off."

"Wait, what? It can do that?" Was there nothing magic couldn't do?

Marilyn threw her head back and laughed. "I'm kidding. I would refrigerate it, though."

Addison was scared to leave the bag in her house. No way was she putting the stinky bandage on before going to a party where she was trying to make friends.

She thanked Marilyn and rushed inside to put the bag inside another bag, inside a box, and put that box inside the fridge. "I want to see something with legs get out of that."

Back to the unpleasant business at hand, she got in her car and drove to her childhood home. She tried to remember her earliest memories, and they all took place in that house with Theresa. Her father had died right after she was born, so she'd never met him. It had been her and Mom against the world for as long as she could remember.

Thankfully, Leo was at work. She didn't want an audience.

She knocked on the front door and went inside. "Mom, you here?"

Theresa popped her head out of the living room. "This is a pleasant surprise. Come on in. I'm looking at paint swatches right now. You can help."

The symbols had been etched deep enough that they had to hire someone to replace all the drywall. The man worked quickly and didn't ask questions. Her kind of contractor.

Five lines of different color paint were along one wall. There was a pastel purple, a mint green, a sky blue, a pinkish rose, and a bright yellow. "Wow. You're all over the place with these."

"Yeah. I liked all of these in the store, so Leo painted them for me so I could see them in the room. He's such a good boy." She sat on the couch and stared at the colors. "So, which one gets your vote?"

Addison sat down and angled her body toward

her mom. "I think you'll be happiest with the rose. That's not why I'm here, though." She set the grimoire down on the coffee table in front of them. No hint of recognition crossed her mother's face.

Theresa opened it and fanned through a couple of pages. "That's a fancy book. Is this related to those symbols?"

If she was lying, she was good. "So you have never been able to read, write, or speak Gaelic?"

Theresa chuckled. "Definitely not. I tried those apps that teach you and I tried both Spanish and French. It turns out I can't retain other languages."

Addison hesitated. "I need to have a difficult conversation with you, and I need you to be completely honest with me. I mean it. I need the truth, no matter how hard it is to admit."

Theresa's eyebrows drew together. "You're scaring me. What's this all about?"

"Is your real name Addison Schmidt?"

Theresa cocked her head. "No. That's your name."

Addison opened the grimoire to the page Luna had translated. Next to it was a printout of what the page said in English. She waited for her mom to read it.

"I don't understand." Her mom genuinely looked confused.

"This book belongs to our family. I'm a witch named Addison, like every other female in our family for generations. Why are you still pretending you don't know what I'm talking about?" Addison had tried to stay calm. It didn't work.

Theresa grabbed her hand and squeezed. "Honey. I swear to you, I've never seen this book before or heard anything about magic in our family."

Addison believed her. That didn't change anything, though. "There has to be some relative out there we can reach out to?"

Theresa frowned. "You know I have no family."

Addison knew the stories. Her mom had been raised in a group home and had been alone except for her brief relationship with Addison's father, who died when Addison was an infant. It was a dead end.

It didn't make sense, though. "I have somewhere I have to go. Tomorrow I'd like to take you to meet my friend Luna. Maybe the truth is blocked inside you like it is with Marilyn."

"I'll do whatever you want. I don't enjoy seeing you like this. I have an appointment in the morning to get my nails done. Let me know where you want me to go after that." She stood up and kissed the top of Addison's head. "Looks like you need to get your roots done again, too."

Addison gasped. "Damn, rude! My own mother, so mean."

"That's what family is for, dear. At least I haven't mentioned the fact that you smell like Febreze." Theresa gave her a pointed look.

"Hey, I've been busy, okay?" Addison hoisted the heavy grimoire off the table. "Have fun with your nails and I'll text you a time and an address."

Tears sprang to her eyes as she walked out. What if Theresa wasn't her mother? They'd both be devastated. That's impossible though, right? A woman knows if she's given birth. Maybe she got switched at birth in the hospital.

No, she wasn't going to think about that right now. Instead, she'll stress over her roots for the entire drive to the secret society meeting. Thanks, Mom.

eighteen

ADDISON PULLED into the parking lot and stared at the unassuming building. Other than the symbol that was on the invitation, there was no indication of what the property was. They were secret, so it made sense their branding would be minimal.

She did as Luna taught her and opened her senses to see if there was anything odd, and gasped when she saw the glow of energy radiating around the building. It was in its own little bubble. That made sense. They probably didn't want random people stumbling into their meeting.

She took one last look at her hair that her mom picked on and went inside. A small woman sat behind a desk in an otherwise empty room. "May I help you?"

Addison held up the invitation. "Oh yes, our new recruit. Right this way." She stood up and walked straight through the wall behind the desk.

"What the hell?" Addison stepped up and studied the wall. It looked solid. Did they assume she knew how to walk through walls? Can all witches walk through walls?

The woman's face appeared through the wall, causing Addison to jump and grab her chest. "For the love of... you scared the crap out of me."

Her unhelpful guide chuckled. "Sorry about that. This wall isn't really here. If any humans walk in, that's all they'll see. Come along."

Her face disappeared again. Addison reached out and brushed the surface. Like the woman said, her fingers went straight through. She felt nothing but air.

"Okay, here goes." She gathered her courage and charged through.

She was met with no resistance and ended up rushing into the room and slamming into a table. Two small men who weren't men sitting at the table grumbled and walked away.

The still unhelpful woman chuckled. "My goodness. You like to make an entrance."

Addison's eyes bulged at her. If she had prepared Addison a little better, she wouldn't have made a fool of herself.

"I'm Hetty and this is *The Order of the Teal Matrons*." She waved her arm dramatically toward the room.

"Seriously Hetty? We told you we're not calling it that. There are men here." A gorgeous man with porcelain skin and fangs yelled across the room.

Fangs... those were fangs. Holy crap. A vampire in real life.

Addison tried to contain her giddy excitement. Every creature she'd ever read about in her paranormal romance and fantasy books was in the room.

Hetty sighed dramatically. "Fine. Welcome to *The Union of the Timeless Accord*." She stuck her tongue out at the man and walked away.

Addison didn't know what to do, so she walked to a table along the wall and grabbed a can of soda. She resisted shuddering at the bottles of blood labeled by type, lined up like the soda was.

A very short man and woman walked up and had to reach for their drinks.

Addison couldn't contain her excitement. "Oh my gosh, are you guys goblins, or trolls?"

The woman gasped. "Excuse me? How rude. We're gnomes. Those are goblins." She pointed to the two men who had been sitting at the table she knocked into earlier.

She felt her face heat. "Oh. Sorry, I'm new to all this."

The couple rolled their eyes and walked away.

Addison was off to a great start. She walked the perimeter, smiling at people as she went and studying the art on the walls. It was scenes of battles and wars with all the creatures involved. She stopped to study a statue of a mummy. "Geez, buddy, what did you do to deserve this?" She mumbled.

The mummy rolled his eyes that she thought were glass. "Maybe I was falsely accused. You ever thought of that?" He turned and hobbled away with his legs that couldn't bend. "Come on Addison, get it together."

A totally human-looking couple walked up. The man pointed at the paintings. "These are here to remind us what will happen if the different races don't work together. Everyone in here is committed to accepting and coexisting with each other."

The woman held her hand out. "I'm Sonya. Before you ask if I'm like a mermaid or something, I'll tell you I'm a witch. This is my husband, Bernard. He's a warlock." A tiny creature popped out from under her hair. "This is Olly, my dragon familiar."

Addison gasped and reached out to touch him. "He's so adorab-" The dragon snapped at her fingers.

Sonya clucked her tongue. "Behave Olly. She doesn't know any better." She looked back at Addison. "Like service animals, you should always ask before touching someone's familiar."

"Of course. I'm so sorry. I'll just go-" She walked backward and through a cold mist.

As she stepped through, the mist reformed as a female ghost. "Watch where you're walking."

"Can someone control her before Veronica turns her into dinner?" The vampire from before shouted. The woman next to him smiled at Addison and licked her lips, her fangs sticking out.

"Don't mind the vampires. They are all *bark*, no *bite*." The ghost of a man in clothing from the eighteen hundreds said next to her ear before throwing his head back and laughing loudly. "Ah, I kill myself."

Addison jumped to the side. A female ghost in a

flapper outfit was on her other side. "You're wound a little tight, honey. Come sit with us."

Rather than be alone, Addison followed them into another room with chairs set up in rows in front of a small stage with a podium on it.

The flapper girl sat in the back row and patted the seat next to her. Addison sat down and the male ghost sat on her other side. She was a ghost sandwich. Her kids were never going to believe her.

"I'm Francesca and this is Alexander."

"Addison." Her attention was caught as paranormals of all kinds filled the room. "So what's happening here?"

"Once a month, we gather here and talk about anything that affects us. Usually, someone from another group can help." Alexander answered.

"Hopefully, this isn't an insensitive question, but how are you two here? I thought ghosts haunted the place where they died. And why don't we see more, like all the time?" Addison had so many questions. Leo was going to be so excited to know he was at least partially right and ghosts do exist.

Francesca chuckled. "No topic is too insensitive for us. Everything is a bit drab as a ghost, so we like it when things get spicy."

That was probably why they were attracted to Addison. She was a walking disaster, after all.

Francesca continued. "Most ghosts do haunt a place. Some can haunt an object. I'm attached to my cigarette holder. That very nice siren over there, Citrine." She pointed to a painfully beautiful woman sitting in the front row. "Found me and has agreed to carry my object with her so I can travel."

"And that Golem over there is named Hank." He pointed to a bulky man hunched over in the third row. "He found my pocket watch and agreed to the same. As to why you don't see more ghosts, it's simple. You see us if we want you to see us."

"Well, that's a neat trick, to hide from anyone whenever you want." How many ghosts were hanging around her house? Did they watch her in the shower or, even worse, when she sat on the couch eating large hunks of raw cookie dough?

"Oh, it's starting. That man," Francesca pointed to a man with pointed ears walking across the stage. "Is Clifford. He's an elf and our unofficial wrangler."

"Okay, okay. Silence. Let's get a move on." Clifford did not sound very enthused about being in charge. "The first order of business, the brownies who live in the trees off 5th Avenue, thank Veronica and Geoff for buying the lot and saving their home from being torn down."

Everyone clapped loudly as the vampires stoically nodded.

"The next order-" Clifford cut in.

"Sir. I have an urgent matter and ask to be heard now instead of waiting until the end?" A man with muscles on his muscles stood against the wall looking around the room, his face pleading to be heard.

Clifford sighed. "Seamus, this is highly irregular, but I'll allow it."

Seamus walked to the front of the room so everyone could see him without having to turn around. "It's about the Malvado sisters," murmurs erupted around the room.

Clifford banged his fist on the podium. "Let him continue."

Seamus nodded. "Three of my pack came home last night severely injured. They said they were spelled by the sisters to guard an old factory and then they said something about machines coming to life and lightning bolts raining down. We've allowed these witches' freedom to cause havoc for too long. Spelling other creatures to do harm is crossing a line. I ask that we take care of them for good."

The murmurs were much louder now as everyone in the room seemed pissed.

Addison jumped up from her seat. "Oh, that was me!" Several people gasped.

"Oh dear, I knew she would be fun," Francesca whispered to Alexander.

"Explain yourself," Clifford demanded.

"The spelling and all that wasn't me. I mean, they were attacking me and my friends. See, the witches had been after my family book. They tracked it to my neighbor's house and then stole her cat, who was apparently her husband cursed to live as a cat, but she didn't know that."

Francesca's cold hand brushed Addison's arm. "Slow down. Take a breath."

Addison did as she was told. With so many eyes on her, she'd started word vomiting. She smiled at the ghost and mouthed thank you. "The witches wanted the cat to tell them where the book was. Unfortunately for them, he didn't know. My friends and I found where they were keeping him and we went to rescue him. When we were leaving, several shifters attacked us. My magic is wonky at best and it was my fault the broken machines attacked them. I won't apologize though. They were trying to hurt us. And it turns out my neighbor, the cat's wife, is a witch. When one of the shifters got a hold of her cat husband, she freaked and sent the lightning bolts down. It's the only reason we escaped." She turned and pulled the shoulder of her dress down to show the four deep claw marks. "We were lucky to get out of there,"

Seamus growled loudly. "They made my pack harm innocent people. Justice must be done."

Cheers of agreement went up around the room.

Sonya, the witch with the adorable but sharp-toothed dragon, raised her hand and stood when Clifford pointed to her. "The coven in Raydell has a serious beef with the sisters. If this order gives permission, they will come in, capture the witches, and bind their magic."

Seamus shook his head. "That's not good enough. We all know they have the death of the Stoker family on their hands. Now they are making others harm for them. Too much blood has been spilled."

Addison paled. She wanted the witches off her back, but this sounded like an execution.

A tiny speck flew up from the shelf on the wall and transformed into a woman with silk wings.

"Wow. That was awesome." Several people

snickered at Addison. She hadn't meant to say that out loud.

The woman nodded at her in thanks and turned to the crowd. "If their magic is bound, the Fae would be willing to imprison them in our world for 100 years."

Okay, prison sounded better than execution. Addison could get on board with that.

Some ogres in the corner continued arguing for death. Blood thirsty, weren't they?

Clifford slapped the podium and got everyone's attention again. "All those in favor of allowing the Raydell coven to bind the Malvado sister's magic and imprisoning them in the Fae realm for the period of 100 years, say Aye."

Everyone in the room raised their hand, fin, or paw in agreement. Addison sat down without voting. She was too new to the world to have any say in what was right or wrong.

Clifford nodded. "A plan has been made. Seamus, I hope this satisfies your pack?"

The wolf leader bowed his head at everyone and went back to his place against the wall.

"As for the second order of business," Clifford continued. "Addison Schmidt."

All eyes turned toward her. She wanted to shrink

to fairy size and hide up on the shelf. She was a big girl, though. She raised her hand. "Present."

"You have caused all manner of chaos these last few months. We've had to do extensive cleanup to keep the humans from looking too close and finding out about our world. This is a very grievous issue. It has been requested that your magic be bound and your memory wiped."

He held up his hand when she gasped. "But Bernard and Sonya believe you are worth rehabilitating."

Bernard stood and turned to her. "If you are in agreement, our coven will send someone to train you."

Addison nodded eagerly. "Please. That would be wonderful. I'm just learning about these powers. I promise I'll try harder to not cause chaos."

"Do we really think she can control herself after sixty years of dormancy?" A sinfully good looking man leaning against the wall asked.

Addison shot to her feet again. "Excuse me, sir. I am only forty-six." She glanced down at Francesca. "I don't look like I'm in my sixties, right?"

Francesca rolled her eyes. "That's Devon, he's a demon. Of course he's going to be insulting. Ignore him. He likes to rile people up."

Clifford saved her from getting into a fight in front of everyone while they were voting on her. Her outburst probably didn't look very good for her. "All those in favor?" Clifford boomed.

Addison wilted in her chair as everyone except the vampires raised their hands. Geez, she hadn't even done anything to them. Maybe later she could send them a bottle of blood or something to make amends. Hopefully Luna would know the protocol and where the heck you even got blood from.

Clifford moved on to the next item on the agenda. Addison couldn't focus, though. She'd almost lost her magic. She didn't know if she really wanted it. That was her decision to make, though. No matter who they sent to help her, she would welcome them eagerly.

nineteen

TODAY WAS EITHER GOING to be one of the worst days of her life or the best. Addison had the day off from work. The witches who were hunting her were being taken care of. She was wearing clean clothes fresh out of the dryer, and she and her mom were going to see Luna.

Her mind was still reeling from the secret society meeting the night before. Her eyes had been opened to a whole new world. She had irked more than a few people, but she also made a few potential friends. Unfortunately, two of them were dead, so that sucked. On the other hand, that meant they would always be around.

Francesca and Alexander had begged their previous handlers to loan their haunted items to

Addison for a while as she was proving to be a huge source of entertainment, their words. She hadn't minded, though she did set the rule that they were never to go in her bedroom or bathroom and the same went for any of her guests. No free peep shows allowed. Francesca had seemed more bummed by the rule than Alexander. Go figure.

Theresa pulled up outside *The Soul Apothecary* and waved her freshly painted nails at Addison. "I've been wanting to check this place out. I wasn't sure if I'd fit in, though."

"Luna is the owner, and she is very sweet. We're just waiting for Xavier. He's helping me figure all this out. And speak of the devil," Addison waved to Xavier as he pulled his truck in on the other side of her car.

"Morning ladies." He opened the door to the store for them. "Addison, I want to hear all about last night. Unless it's so secret you can't say?"

Addison bit her lip as she thought back. "You know, they didn't swear me to secrecy or threaten me if I told anyone. I think the secret part is from humans and while you are a human, you already know all about this world, so I think we're good."

Luna popped her head up from behind a counter of leather bound journals. "Are you guys talking about the meeting? I want to hear too. Come to the table. I'll bring coffee."

Theresa gawked at everything as Addison pulled her along. Luna came back with four cups of coffee and sat down. "Spill the deets."

Addison held up a finger as she chugged. She'd been so nervous to get here and talk about her mom that she'd run right out without her gross microwave coffee. "Okay. That was really freaking hot." She fanned her mouth. "Phew, so, the big news is we no longer have to worry about the witches from the other night. Long story short, they were the Malvado sisters and have been causing trouble for a long time. There was some insinuation that they have killed people before. They had spelled those shifters into working for us. The society voted and a neighboring coven who hates the sisters is coming in to bind their magic. The Fae agreed to imprison them in their realm for 100 years."

No one spoke as she finished talking. In fairness, it was a lot to take in.

"Oh, and these are my new friends Francesca and Alexander." The two ghosts appeared behind her. Xavier jumped at the same time Luna yelped, and her mother gasped. She pointed at Theresa.

"Don't mention this to the boys. I want to surprise them at dinner tonight."

Theresa nodded, her mouth still hung open in shock.

"Good morning everyone. I'm so happy to make your acquaintance." Alexander pointed at Xavier and smiled. "A man with style. So rare these days."

Francesca held her hand up and waved her fingers. "I'm so excited to be here. If you guys are as fun as Addison, we'll be fast friends."

Luna pouted. "No fair. Why wasn't I invited to the meeting? I want ghost friends too."

"Well, I wasn't exactly welcome. Apparently, I had been on their radars for a while because of all my screwups. They voted whether to take my magic away and erase my memory. There's a coven here in town and they offered to teach me enough to stop being a nuisance. So I guess I'm on some kind of probation."

Xavier whistled. "That sounds like it was an intense meeting."

"You have no idea. I'm pretty sure a couple of vampires want to drain me."

Francesca nodded enthusiastically. "It's true. She really annoyed them."

"Oh, and a demon, like from Hell, told everyone

in the room I was in my sixties." Addison was still pissed about that.

Theresa reached over and covered Addison's hand with hers. "My poor baby."

The reminder of why they were there fell like a lead balloon in Addison's stomach. "Speaking of... Luna, I was wondering what you saw with my mom's aura. She swears she's not Addison and not magical."

Luna sat back and studied Theresa. "She's right. She's not magic. There's not a drop in her. However, she has been touched by magic. She has the same thick black shroud over her that Marilyn has. I'd bet the same person did both."

Tears sprang to Addison's eyes. That could only mean one thing.

Xavier leaned forward. "While we figure out how to remove these blocks, we should go the human route and do a DNA test. That will be a definitive answer."

Theresa slapped her hand on the table. "What are you both talking about? Addison is my daughter. I am her mother. All of this is nonsense. I would know if I didn't have a child." Tears poured down her cheeks.

Addison leaned over and hugged her. "It doesn't

matter what any test or book says, you're right, you are my mother." She sat back and wiped her own wet cheeks. She didn't need the test to know Theresa wasn't her biological mom.

She couldn't stop, though. She needed to know where her real mom was and how she got separated from her. Damn, perimenopause had to come along and unlock her magic. She was blissfully ignorant before. A large part of her thought maybe she should have her magic bound and her memory wiped. They could go back to being a normal family.

That was the easy way out. If nothing else was true about Addison, it was that she never did anything easy.

Now the question was... Where is Addison Schmidt?

twenty

ADDISON STARED out her living room window. "Now remember, don't reveal yourselves right away. I want to really surprise the kids." Addison was so excited for her boys to meet Alexander and Francesca.

"Do you want us to move stuff around and make sounds to really throw them off?" Alexander looked at her hopefully.

She thought about it and then shrugged. "Maybe a little. Let's not get too crazy. We've had a rough few weeks."

The sound of car doors closing drew her attention back to the window. "They're here."

The ghosts disappeared in an instant. That really was a neat trick.

Fitz knocked and then opened the front door. Leo and Iggy were right behind him. Each took a turn hugging her.

Iggy sniffed. "Why do you smell funny?"

Addison forgot she had used Marilyn's poultice earlier that morning. Three showers later and she could still get a faint whiff of the putrid stench whenever she moved her arm. "Marilyn and I are kind of having a truce. It turns out she's good with herbs. I had a sore shoulder, and she made me an ointment to put on it."

Fitz raised an eyebrow. "You and Marilyn? You have a truce?"

"Crazier things have happened."

Leo slapped the back of his neck and turned to look in the air above him. "I felt something land on me."

A door down the hall slammed shut. "Is someone here?" Fitz asked.

This was more fun than Addison should admit. "Nope. Must have been the air pressure from opening the front door." She turned toward the kitchen and waved them on. "Come on. I'm cooking."

"Wait-"

"No-."

"You've got to be joking."

She turned around and gaped at them. "Geez guys. You forget, I used to always cook for you."

Leo continued swatting at the air around him as if a fly was bothering him. "Sure, that was before. Now you are more likely to burn the house down than cook a meal."

Fitz's keys landed with a hard thud on the wood floor, making everyone jump. He bent down to grab them. "How the heck did these fall out of my pocket?"

"Look. I have everything laid out. I just need to prepare it. You guys can hang out and dinner will be ready soon." She turned around to chop carrots when all three boys shouted at the same time.

She spun around and burst into laughter. Her trusty wooden spoon that was usually her weapon was now dancing quite animatedly across the kitchen.

"Is this your magic?" Leo asked as he waved the air around the spoon, looking for strings. "I mean, I know you said you had it. Actually, seeing it though, is crazy."

She wiped the tears from her eyes as she laughed. "Okay, guys. That's enough."

The boys looked at each other, confused.

Francesca appeared in front of them, holding the spoon. Alexander appeared at their feet. He was almost finished tying all three boy's shoes to each other. "I was almost finished."

She had never seen her boys move so fast. They took off running, tripping as they went with their partially tied shoes.

"Guys wait. It's okay." Addison hugged her side. She had a cramp from laughing so hard.

They stopped at the front door and turned back to look at her.

"You guys are seeing a man and a woman standing next to Ma, right?" Leo asked.

Fitz and Iggy nodded silently.

"These are my new friends, Alexander and Francesca. They're ghosts I met at the meeting last night." The specters waved to the boys.

"It's very nice to meet you." Alexander gave a small bow.

"We were having a little fun. We didn't mean to scare you." Francesca added.

Leo smoothed down his shirt. "You didn't scare me. I didn't want the other two embarrassed, so I went along with it." He walked up and held his hand out to her. "I'm Leo."

Addison rolled her eyes. "Down boy. She's dead."

To prove her point, Francesca reached out to shake his hand. Hers went right through his.

"Woah. It's cold, just like they say in the movies."

Fitz and Iggy walked back. They still looked unsure.

Addison waved to the couches. "Why don't you all sit down and get to know each other while I finish dinner?"

Leo sat quickly on the loveseat and patted the seat next to him. "You can sit here Francesa."

"Bro." Fitz sighed.

"Dude," Iggy whispered.

Addison hadn't expected one of her boys falling for a ghost. This was all new territory for all of them.

She watched the five of them talk animatedly for a few minutes. She'd been all but forgotten. "Guess you don't mind if I cook?"

Two waved her off, and the third didn't even answer.

It had been a long time since she'd cooked a full meal for multiple people. There was so much to do.

Maybe a little magic would help. She'd been reading and practicing. Surely she wouldn't start another fire.

She stared at the knife on the counter next to the

vegetables and willed it to chop them. She opened the fridge door and hid behind it in case the knife went flying. After a few seconds, she peeked around and saw it actually dicing the tomato. "Okay. I got this."

She looked at the mixer. "Turn on." The whisk attachment spun, blending the cake mix.

She turned to grab the steaks out of the fridge and cocked her head at the woman standing in the doorway. "Oh hello. Are you Iggy's girlfriend, Serenity? He didn't tell me you were coming."

Addison held her hand out. She was a little surprised that the woman looked a few years older than her son.

The woman crossed her arms. "I'm not with Iggy." She clucked her tongue. "You know, using magic for such mundane tasks is beneath you."

"I'm sorry. Are you friends with Leo or Fitz?"

She shook her head. "I'm not their friend. I'm yours."

Crazy lady says what?

"I'm happy to make new friends, but I don't think we've met."

"I'm your emotional support witch, Minnie."

"What the hell is an emotional support witch?" Addison was thoroughly confused.

A beautiful smile spread across Minnie's face. "You'll find out."

Ready to find out who Addison's mom is? Book Two, Hexes and Hijinks releases July 9th, 2024.
Keep reading for a sneak peek.

Addison stared at the envelope in her hands. This was it. The DNA results were in. Her mother, Theresa, had said she didn't want to know the results. Addison didn't blame her. She would give anything to roll back a month and forget everything she'd learned. She didn't want to blow her family up.

It had to be done though. If a whole line of Addison Schmidt's had come before her, she owed it to them to learn the truth.

She blew out a breath and ripped the envelope open. She silently read the results and then read them again.

Maybe she was misinterpreting something, so she read it a third time.

There it was, in black and white. Theresa was not her biological mother. So, who was?

She felt so alone.

"Hey Addison, the Netflix has paused again," Alexander shouted from the living room.

Well, not completely alone.

Francesca and Alexander were ghosts she'd met at the secret society meeting. They liked her so much they asked to come home with her. She'd accidentally showed them Netflix and they've been on a binge for days. Apparently, ghosts don't sleep.

She still had the letter in her hand when she went to the couch and pushed the button to have the show play again. "You know, when my kids were little, I made them play outside one hour for every two hours of video game and television time."

Francesca looked up from the TV. "What's wrong? You sound like something's wrong." She tilted her head and read the results. "Oh, honey. I'm so sorry."

There was a brief knock at the front door.

"Come on in." Minnie had texted Addison she was on her way over with news.

Her coven appointed emotional support witch breezed in. "Morning everyone. Oh, season three is a good one." She turned and caught sight of Addison's face. "I'm guessing you got confirmation about what we already knew?"

Addison was still trying to get used to Minnie's sarcasm. "Something this big needed confirmation."

Minnie nodded. "Let's go in the kitchen so we don't disturb these two."

It didn't look like a bomb exploding would disturb the two ghosts. They were practically fused to the couch.

Addison nuked two cups of coffee and sat down. "I hope your news is better than mine was?"

Minnie smiled brightly. "Actually, it is. As you know, Marilyn came to a coven meeting the other night, and we weren't able to break the shroud over her. Sonya talked to the Raydell coven and they've agreed to join with us to try again. They are a bigger and stronger coven. We'll unblock Marilyn and your mother, and then you can settle down and focus on your studies. It's not enough to be born into a magical family."

Addison ignored the jab. It wasn't her fault she came from a long line of insanely powerful witches.

"On that note, should we get some practice in?"

Addison glanced at the clock on the microwave. "Sure. I don't have a lot of time, though. It's Fitz's birthday and I still need to get his present sorted out."

Minnie rolled her eyes, but kept her thoughts to herself. "Did you read the book on the elements?"

Addison nodded. "Having the ghosts absorbed in the TV has given me lots of quiet time. I think I'm connected to the fire element, given I keep setting fires."

Minnie waved her hand and four objects appeared on the table. "Magic isn't always logical. It's not safe to assume anything. Let's see how you do with these. The feather is to test air, the seed for

Earth, the candle for fire, and the glass of water is obviously for water."

The witch had the gall to back up against the counter and conjure a police riot shield.

Addison lifted one eyebrow. "Really?"

Minnie shrugged. "I've seen what you can do. Better to be safe than sorry."

Emotional support witch probably wasn't the right term for Minnie. She was more of an emotional toughening witch.

"Look at the four objects and start with whichever one is calling to you."

Addison nodded and took her time studying each item. Fire had to be her element. She stared at the wick, imagining it lighting. Her intent was obvious. Maybe too obvious there was a hint of smoke a second before a raging blast of fire shot up, almost reaching the ceiling, and melted the candle into a puddle of wax.

Minnie chuckled as she waved her hand and put out the fire. "Not surprised there. Are any of the others calling to you?"

Addison stared at the glass of water. She meant to send the water swirling like a tornado. Instead, the faucet turned on, and a stream of water stretched across the room and filled the cup to overflowing. She scooted back when the water ran over the table and toward the floor.

Minnie waved her hand again, and the chaos stopped. "Interesting. Anything else?"

For a minute she stared at the seed. What was her intention supposed to be with that? In her mind, she pictured a small rose unfurling from it.

The little seed danced around like a kernel about to turn into popcorn when suddenly it split open. A rose came out, along with ten more and vines which were snaking their way toward her. One of them wrapped around her wrist and another was going for her neck.

Minnie did her 'fix Addison's chaos' hand wave. "A little bloodthirsty, aren't you? Not sure what your intention was there."

Addison's hands were still around her throat, where the vine had choked her. "Really? You think I would intend for anything even remotely like that?"

"You are a strange woman whom I barely know. How am I supposed to know what you're thinking? Now, try the feather."

Addison concentrated on making the feather lift gently into the air. She wilted in relief that nothing bad happened.

A screech from the living room was her first indication something was wrong. Before she could get up to investigate, several pillows came flying into the room and landed on the table. Something was moving inside them. "I don't think I want to know what that is." A shudder racked her body as she pictured worms or snakes slithering in a big ball of horribleness.

Suddenly there was a ripping sound as small holes were made in the pillows and feathers flew out and floated around the room.

Addison wilted against the chair. "Oh, thank god. I was imagining so much worse."

"You do make a mess, don't you?"

Addison turned to say something snarky back. A snort-laugh escaped her before she covered her mouth. A majority of the feathers had flown at Minnie and were sticking to her. She looked like Big Bird's little sister.

"Oh no. I swear I didn't mean to do that." She wiped the tears from her eyes as Minnie shook the feathers off and sat down at the table.

"Well, it would seem you have a connection to all four elements. You may still have one stronger than the rest. We'll figure that out as we go." She tapped her nails on the table as she studied Addison.

"I've never met anyone connected to more than two. Your family must be incredibly powerful."

Excitement coursed through Addison. If you're going to be a witch, why not be a super-powered one? What's the worst that could happen?

Book Two, Hexes and Hijinks releases July 9th, 2024.

about the author

Cassidy and her family recently relocated to the North Georgia Mountains after a lifetime in the Tampa Bay, Florida area. She's on a new adventure and loving every minute of it.

She loves reading and going to the movies, but not nearly as much as she enjoys traveling and hopes to one day watch a baseball game in every MLB stadium in the country.

She also writes under the pen name C.K. O'Connor. Books by C.K. range from sweet romance to young adult to historical romance.

To learn more about C.K. / Cassidy please visit her online at

www.cassidykoconnor.com.

You can also find her on Facebook at

https://www.facebook.com/CK-OConnor-Author-101376192171379

OR

www.facebook.com/cassidykoconnorauthor

other books by cassidy

<u>Paranormal Investigative Services Series</u>

Faeted under Fire

Stitched Under Fire

Taken Under Fire

Nightshade Guild Series

Mated To A Mage

Magic Burned

Swing Time

Crimson Moon Hideaway

Bearly Healed

The Fast and The Furry

Love Possessed

<u>Black Hollow Series</u>

Loving the Monster Within

Reviving Love

Sacrificing Love

Accepting Love

Resisting Love

Mending Love

<u>Forgiving Love</u>

<u>Fearing Love</u>

<u>Stand Alones</u>

Gruff Love

Sexy In White

To Steal a Prince's Heart

Wicked Wonderland Retreat Box Set

www.ingramcontent.com/pod-product-compliance
Lightning Source LLC
Chambersburg PA
CBHW070503200726
48293CB00007B/2353